HUNTER/PREY

Sam Sisavath

Hunter/Prey
Copyright © 2015 by Sam Sisavath

Published by Road to Babylon Media
Visit www.roadtobabylon.com for news, updates, and announcements

Edited by Jennifer Jensen and Wendy Chan
Cover by Creative Paramita
Formatting by BB eBooks

ISBN-13: 978-0692368282
ISBN-10: 0692368280

Revenge means carrying a loaded shotgun.

She has been planning this for ten years. She's thought of everything and trained for this one single night. Nothing could possibly go wrong.

He's a serial killer who has eluded the police for the last ten years. When his latest victim turns out to not be who she appears, the hunter will discover what it's like to be the prey.

When these two very determined foes clash, there **will** be blood. One way or another, only one of them is coming out of this alive...

"Before you embark on a journey of revenge, dig two graves."

—Confucius

CHAPTER 1

HE WAS GOING to kill her, there was no doubt about that. That was, after all, the whole point of tonight for the both of them. The question was: Who wanted to kill the other more?

He took her with the kind of practiced ease that could only come from having done it many times before: Running her car off the highway, yanking her from her seat before she even had a chance to recover from the crash, and then throwing her to the ground. All of that was to show her he meant business. He needn't have gone the extra mile; she knew his intentions as soon as he began ramming his truck into her back bumper.

He pounced quickly, so quickly. She hadn't expected that, and it threw her timing off until she realized that everything had worked out just as she had planned—which was both exhilarating and horrifying.

He's done this so, so many times before, she thought as he threw her to the soft, damp ground. It had rained yesterday, and the wetness seeped through her jeans and blouse instantly. Thank God it wasn't as slippery as it could have been; she was going to need every bit of her agility against a man his size.

"Don't fight it; it's just going to make things worse," he said.

Or hissed. This beast in man's clothing. He even looked monstrous against the canvas of moonlight pouring through the trees around them.

"No," she said, the word coming out as a loud gasp.

The heavy breathing, the feel of drowning, wasn't part of the plan. She really did find it difficult to breathe at the moment because this was it. This was the night she had been waiting for.

Ten years of research, six years of training, and three years of getting ready for this moment.

God help me.

"I know who you are," she said. Those words came out easier. Much, much easier.

It was all going according to plan. Mostly.

Ten years of research...

She could see it on his face. He hadn't expected that response. She knew what he was waiting for—begging, crying, smeared makeup, and groveling at his feet. When he didn't get any of those things, he cocked his head to one side as if to get a better view of her.

"Who are you?" he asked.

"I'm exactly everything you wanted," she said, and kicked out with her right leg, connecting with his crotch. It was such a "girl move," as one of her instructors would say, but given her current position—on the ground, with him hovering over her—it was the most viable and effective option open to her.

...six years of training...

Before he could gather himself, she grabbed a handful of dirt and threw it in his face. He batted at it awkwardly, the knife gripped tightly in his right hand (*Where the hell did that come from?*) gleaming in the moonlight. The blade was long and sharp, with a serrated section for tough cutting.

She scrambled to her feet and dived forward, back toward the car, aiming right at the open driver-side door. She didn't go for the keys dangling from the ignition. Instead, she grabbed the lever next to the seat and yanked it, heard the *pop!* as the trunk opened in the back, the soft, metallic echo like a ringing bell against the quiet countryside.

He was wincing, parts of his eyes still clogged with dirt while simultaneously trying to fight through the pain from between his legs. Girl move or not, men lived in mortal fear of getting kicked in the scrotum because it *hurt*.

She pulled away from the open door and backpedaled along the length of the vehicle. She gave herself a brief second or two to enjoy the confusion clouding his eyes (they were light brown, but she didn't know how much of that was dirt) as he attempted to follow her movements while the mind behind them tried in vain to understand what she was doing—why she was still here and why she hadn't tried to flee yet.

...and three years of getting ready for this moment...

By the time he gathered himself and took his first stumbling step after her, she was already at the back of the car, reaching into the open trunk. She pulled back the rug, ignored the spare tire, and went right for the pump-action shotgun hidden inside its compartment.

It was a Remington model, the kind used by cops around the country. The guy who had sold it to her, then taught her how to use it over the course of two months for a flat fee, said the SWAT guys liked carrying it for the firepower and accuracy. Training on the weapon had caused her a lot of bruises and painful mornings, but she had gotten good at it. When she put her mind on achieving something, there were few things in this universe that could stop her.

He must have sensed that something had gone wrong, because when she stepped away from the trunk with the shotgun, he had already paused his pursuit of her. By the time she reappeared in the open, revealing herself (and the shotgun in her hands), he had already turned around and was running in the other direction.

She fired.

The flames that stabbed out of the Remington's barrel lit up the darkened woods for less than a second and illuminated the sight of him darting to his right and over the hood of the car. He was sliding across the vehicle as she ran after him, racking the shotgun as she went, and fired again.

The driver-side window exploded and the *ping-ping!* of buckshot slamming into the side of the Ford echoed back and forth against the trees, the gunshot ear-splitting against the quiet night. She hoped the noise didn't go further than the woods. She didn't need strangers butting in on them right now. Not yet. Not until she had finished what she had come here to do.

Ten years of research, six years of training, and three years of getting ready for this moment...

The man wasn't on the hood anymore. He had probably dropped down on the other side. Which was slick of him. Like something out of a TV show about a couple of brothers and an old souped-up car. Something about Dukes...

She skirted around the vehicle, racking another shell into the shotgun as she did so. Her finger anxiously tested the trigger as she moved sideways, feeling her way without looking. Then she finally circled the hood and lifted the shotgun, ready to fire—

—except there was nothing on the other side to shoot at.

He was gone.

She spun in a circle, searching the woods around her, chest tightening.

Shit.

Shit, shit, shit!

They were less than twenty yards from the state highway, but light out here was scarce except for the generous glow of the moon above. One of her vehicle's headlights was still working, but it was shining in the wrong direction. Both of her taillights had gone out about the fifth time he rammed his truck into them.

She could barely see, much less make out the trees from the branches from the shadows. And if she couldn't see, she couldn't shoot. And if she couldn't shoot, then all of this would be for nothing.

Ten years...

She hurried back around the hood of the Ford to the driver-side door. She slipped inside and used the ceiling light to reach across the seats, opened the glove compartment, and came back out with a heavy Maglite. She clicked it on, the bright LED beam showering the woods around her and illuminating what was once hidden.

She had light now, but he was gone. Disappeared into the darkness. She turned the beam left, right, then all around her.

He was gone.

Just like that, he was gone.

She ran the flashlight along the Ford to gauge the damage. Thin tendrils of smoke were still rising from the corners of the hood, which had lifted like crumpled paper when she hit a tree a

few yards back and spun briefly before finally coming to rest.
The engine had shut down, though she couldn't remember if she
had done that.

The sound of the sleeping woods was suffocating, with the
only out-of-place noise being the slightly chaotic thrumming in
her chest.

Then she saw it, and suddenly everything seemed to get
instantly better.

There was blood on the hood of the car. A large trail of it
slashing from left to right where he had slid across during his
escape—not unscathed, after all.

She trained her flashlight back on the woods and smiled.

"You can run, but you can't hide!" she shouted, just barely
able to contain her rising excitement.

CHAPTER 2

A PART OF him wanted to laugh. Out loud, even.

LOL, amirite?

How could he not? All his life had been spent chasing and stalking and taking people, and here he was stumbling through the woods *(Where the hell am I, anyway?)* while bleeding like a stuck pig. He had seen other people lying, sitting, or running while looking like stuck pigs, but seeing himself (or well, as much of himself as he could see in the semidarkness, anyway) was quite the experience.

Not necessarily a good one, unfortunately.

It would be funny if it weren't so tragic. The younger him wouldn't have fallen for this; but then again, that was a smarter, quicker, and hungrier him. This present him—the one trying to keep himself from bleeding to death—was older but not necessarily wiser. Most damning of all, he had become overconfident and too pleased with himself.

He had gotten sloppy.

Lazy and old and stupid and sloppy.

What was that old saying? *Pride comes before the fall.*

Or maybe it was more like, *You get old, you get lazy, and you get ambushed by a girl.*

He might have actually laughed that time.

Or, at least, a small chuckle, possibly.

He stopped for a moment and took in his surroundings.

What was he doing? He didn't even know where he was going and was literally bumbling around in the dark. He just had to get away from there, that's all.

Where did that shotgun come from?

She must have had it in the trunk the whole time. He remembered seeing her diving into the driver-side door and expecting her to reach for the key and try to drive off. It wouldn't have worked. He was faster, and he would have grabbed her legs before she could even lunge all the way into the vehicle. He was even looking forward to it when he saw her making the leap.

But instead, she had gone for the lever. The trunk lever!

Now that had thrown him off. Big time.

Then the shotgun…

The whole thing wasn't even supposed to go down this far up the highway. The spot where he had prepared to take her was two miles back down the road. But she had proven too resourceful. He should known something was wrong the moment he tried to knock her off the road and she didn't lose control of her vehicle. That should have been his first tip-off. No one drove that well unless they had some training.

Or a lot of training.

All the signs were there; he just hadn't seen them.

Suckered by a girl. This would be embarrassing if anyone knew what I did with my free time.

He had dismissed the possibility that she was a cop and that all of this was one elaborate sting to catch him. Cops had to follow proper police procedure, like reading you your Miranda rights before they pumped you full of buckshot.

No. He had a feeling this was personal.

A grudge.

Or a vendetta.

Same difference? Maybe. He was hurting too much to start doing the semantics dance right now.

He could imagine telling the boys about how a girl had tricked him. Lured him right into a trap like the big ol' dummy he was. Because that's what he felt like at the moment. A big ol' lumbering, bleeding dumb—

Where was I going again?

No idea. This wasn't part of the plan. Far, far from it.

There was no doubt about it. He was lost. All the woods looked the same at night, all the trees identical to the million other trees in the area. There were no signs, no hiking trails, and definitely no roads or buildings to help shed light on his current whereabouts. Unlike the spot he had picked out, everything here was new to him.

He was certain of one thing, though: his truck was behind him, and the highway after that. Of course, there was a woman with a shotgun—and, from all signs, the will and skills to use it—between him and freedom.

Nope. That's definitely not going to work.

Man, he was getting old. Slowing down. About three years ago, he had almost pulled the trigger and called it quits. But no, he had to come back. Because he couldn't stop it. Couldn't temper it, no matter how hard he tried. The girls, the one-night stands, even the widow with the kids had only been temporary buffers.

And then she showed up.

Perfect. So, so perfect.

Suckered by a girl.

Well, goddamn.

He had stopped moving some time ago and hadn't realized it. The root of a tree had caught the tip of his boot and snagged him in place. That drew another short chuckle out of him. The old him wouldn't have let something as minor as a root sticking out of the ground impede his progress. Then again, the younger him wasn't bleeding right now.

The blood…

He looked behind him.

Shit. How had he not noticed that before?

Even under the limited moonlight, he could see still-glistening red drops following him all the way from the highway, a long, jagged trail that just about anyone could follow if they had eyes. The leather fabric of his right glove, pressed against the wound in his side, was sloppily drenched with his own blood.

Snap!

His head whipped around. Too fast; a jolt of pain ripped through his body. He swam through it anyway and stared, barely breathing, waiting for the inevitable. Maybe it was just his imagination, but he swore he heard branches snapping from behind him. Had she found him already? Her and that shotgun?

She had the shotgun in the trunk the whole time. Christ, she knew what she was doing, all right.

There was nothing back there.

At least, nothing *(no one)* that he could see.

Of course, it was so dark…

He trudged on, forcing his legs to move one at a time. He had to keep going because she would be coming. He knew that for a fact. She hadn't set all of this up to give up now, especially when she had the upper hand. And as hard as it was to admit, she was in control here.

Her and that shotgun of hers...

He gripped the knife tighter, comforted by its presence. Ten inches of magnificent, sharp stainless steel. Fifteen inches in all, with a rubberized metal handle at the end. It was an extremely efficient weapon and easy to toss and replace later from an online store. This one was exactly twenty-four months old. Of course, the knife could have been thirty feet long, and it still wouldn't make a difference if she caught him.

Who brings a knife to a shotgun fight? You big dummy.

He flexed his hand over the wound. The blood had seeped through the glove material, and it was warm and sticky against his fingers. For some reason, he always assumed his own blood would feel different against his skin, but it was just the same as all the others he had taken in the past.

Should have retired.

Now look at you, wandering around in the woods at night like a lost old man.

Get off my lawn!

He was pretty sure he actually laughed out loud that time. Maybe, even, LMAO.

CHAPTER 3

THE TRUCK WAS big and black and shiny. The front grill was outfitted to take on lesser-size vehicles, and although her back bumper was a twisted wreck, there was barely any noticeable damage on his hood. Staring at it (was something like this even legal?), she thought it was a minor miracle she had managed to stay on the road and drag the chase out for as long as she had.

The driver-side door had been left open, and inside she found an empty can of Red Bull in the cup holder. The key was nowhere to be found and the ceiling light had turned off, so she had to use the Maglite to sift through the glove compartment. There was a roll of paper towels inside, an unopened pack of gum, and a pair of brand new black leather gloves. There was no insurance paper or ID, nothing that would tell her who he was.

Not that it mattered. She knew exactly who he was even if she didn't know his name. That was superfluous information she could find out after he was dead and she had finished hauling his lifeless corpse to the nearest police station.

She crawled out of the truck. The vehicle was buried deep enough in the woods that it was hidden from the highway nearby. The black paint would help to keep it mostly invisible for the rest of the night and early morning, though an alert passerby would easily spot it in the morning.

Have to finish it before then.

That was always the plan, anyway. She had always given herself one night to do everything she needed to do. After that, it might be difficult to keep the authorities at bay even in this part of the country.

Now all she had to do was find him, and then she could go back to her life. Or what passed for one. She was being overly generous calling it a life. Most of the past decade had been consumed with finding him, luring him, and killing him. After that...

Well, she'd figure that one out later.

Right now, there was just the hunt, and she swore she could *smell* his blood in the air. Was this what it was like for him when he stalked his prey? Was she slipping into his skin without realizing it?

That thought should have terrified her, but instead it gave her a surge of renewed energy.

She went back to her car and pulled the gym bag out of the backseat. She leaned the shotgun against the Ford and took out the black cargo pants and gray T-shirt and put them on. The black wool-knitted sweater finished off her wardrobe change, and she shoved the jeans and blouse into the bag. Finally, she swapped the leather loafers for a pair of black Nike sneakers.

She closed the car door and locked it back up, which made her smile when she saw the broken driver-side window.

The shotgun had six spare rounds in the shell carrier along its side, and she reloaded the weapon now. Then she swapped her large Maglite for a more portable version and grabbed a roll of duct tape from the bag. She fastened the flashlight against the barrel of the shotgun and wrapped it into place, then flicked it on.

One night to finish this.

Get it done!

It didn't take very long to pick up his bloody trail. The Maglite was ridiculously bright, and she shone it across the woods just in case he had retraced his steps and attempted a full-frontal attack to reclaim the upper hand. That was unlikely, though; he was hurt and bleeding and was probably only armed with the knife, or otherwise he would have stayed and fought her if he had a gun on him. But it was better to be safe than sorry. Especially when she was dealing with a man who was more beast than human.

She started off, moving as quietly as she could while still picking up her pace with each step.

The world around her got darker the further she journeyed away from the highway. Without any source of light other than the moonlight and her LED beam to guide her, she became quickly aware of every sound around her, including the ones she made. She was at least comforted by the fact that she had it better than him. He hadn't been carrying a flashlight when he made his escape, or at least none that she had seen.

And besides, she had the shotgun. It didn't matter how big or fast or tough you were. Everyone was reduced to *dead* against a loaded shotgun. It was the reason she had chosen it instead of a handgun. Up close and personal, there was nothing more devastating.

She glanced at her watch: 9:16 P.M.

The loud rumbling of a vehicle behind her made her freeze

in place and look over her shoulder. Bright lights flashed by along the road—just for a split second before the semitrailer disappeared up the state highway, taking its lights with it. She stayed still until the vehicle was little more than a slight hum in the universe...then it was gone, and she was once again alone with the woods and her slightly elevated breathing to keep her company.

She faced forward again and changed up her grip on the Remington. It was a heavy gun—almost eight pounds and eighteen inches long. The matted black color made it ideal for night hunting, and you wouldn't know it existed until it started spitting fire. *Dragon breath*, the ex-cop who had trained her on the weapon called it. The most difficult part of firing a shotgun was the recoil. Learning how to quickly and efficiently rack it using the forend also took some effort. In the end, it was all about repetition and determination. Luckily, she had the time and willpower to commit both.

The blood splatter had no real trajectory, so she guessed he was just stumbling his way through the woods. Which made sense. Not allowing him to force her off the road two miles back had pulled him away from whatever plan he had set up. Maybe he had even picked out a place and gotten familiar with it.

That was the point, after all. They were both in unknown territory now, so that made them even.

Well, not really, because she had the shotgun.

She stopped again. The bloody drops had gotten smaller and were appearing at longer intervals. They had also started to take a noticeably right angle. She stood perfectly still and listened, trying to pick up any noise besides the chirping of birds above her and the scurrying of animals along the branches and among the bushes, reacting to her and his presence.

Nothing. There was nothing.

So where was he going?

Then she heard something that made her turn her head slightly.

It sounded like a laugh.

Or a chuckle.

A trick? Was he was lying in wait for her somewhere out there, hoping to draw her over?

He wasn't stupid. Careless and too sure of himself, yes, but then she had gone to great lengths to put him into that state of mind. But most of it was probably his own doing: All those victims, all those times he had gotten away with it, no doubt played a heavy part in his overconfidence.

She had to be even more careful from this moment on. She had been operating on automatic pilot for the last few minutes, filled with bravado and thinking *she* was the hunter and not the prey. He could change all that in a heartbeat.

Besides, she could afford to be deliberate. She had a whole night to finish him off. How far could he go in his current state? He was a wounded animal, and from all the evidence she'd seen so far, she had gotten him pretty good. A hospital was out of the question. Gunshot wounds were reported to the police, and as much as she didn't need the authorities out here screwing things up, he wanted that even less. Questions always led to more questions, and once the cops looked into his past, it would be game over regardless of how careful he had been over the last ten years.

No. This was going to end with one of them dead at the other's hands. She knew that without a single doubt in her mind.

She started off again, this time at a slower pace, keeping her eyes moving and never on one spot for more than a second each time. Her ears were attuned to any and every noise around and above and to the sides of her.

He was out there, somewhere, and she would find him.

One night.

One night to finish this...

CHAPTER 4

HE WAS GETTING progressively worse, and the dizzying spells were coming faster and lingered longer. His footing was more treacherous than he remembered from a few minutes ago and it took a lot of effort just to swing one leg forward, then start the process all over again with the other one.

Repeat, suck in a breath, and repeat again.

The entire time, he swore he could hear her coming.

So this is what it feels like to be hunted.

Again, he almost laughed out loud. But he couldn't because that would take too much effort and he was simply too weak, even after he had lessened the blood loss. Or, well, had done his best to, anyway. It was hard to see where he was going and twice as difficult to know what he was doing. His hand could be at the wrong spot at this very moment, for all he knew.

He kept moving, because to stop now would be to die. And he didn't want to die. He had too many things left to do, too many goals unfulfilled. And he so, so wanted to fulfill them.

So he stumbled, and staggered, and groped at trees to keep from keeling over. He couldn't take his other hand away from his waist. That was the only thing keeping the rest of his life

from pouring out to the damp ground in a big puddle of dead.
He pulled back his long-sleeve shirt and squinted at his
watch. It had glowing neon hands, but for some reason that
didn't seem to help at the moment. It took him much longer
than necessary (maybe thirty seconds?) to finally pick out the
hour from the minute hand.

9:35 P.M.

Christ. That was it? How long had he been stumbling around
in here? Apparently not very long. Go figure.

He pushed off the tree and took two steps forward when he
heard the *snap!* of a twig and twisted around. Too fast *(Christ, not
again!)* and a bolt of flesh-rendering electricity rippled across his
body for the fifth time in as many...minutes? Seconds?

He grimaced through the pain and had to grab at a tree
trunk—missed it, groped for it again, and managed to get a
handhold on the third try.

He glanced back and stood perfectly still and listened.

Footsteps.

He was sure of it.

Getting closer!

He turned around and began running, ignoring the shooting
pain because even that was better than getting shot.

Of course she had tracked him. How could she not? A blind
man could have followed all the blood he had left in his wake.
And as well prepared as she had been, it was a good bet she'd
probably brought a flashlight along, too.

Come into my web, said the spider to the fly...

She had certainly baited him easily enough. But then, he had
always been a sucker for a city girl. He just didn't know she had
come with a shotgun in the trunk. Though, he had to admit,

even if he had known that…maybe…maybe he would still have gone for it. That was just the kind of guy he was.

He found himself smiling despite the pain.

Maybe, after all this time, he had finally found the one he was looking for. It was too bad she was trying to kill him. But then, what relationship didn't have its problems, especially in the beginning? How could you hope to grow as a couple without weathering a rocky storm or two?

THE LIGHT BECKONED to him between two of the largest trees he had ever laid eyes on. Or maybe that was just the lightheadedness messing with his perception of things. Even the light could have been a figment of his imagination. He hoped not, because he could almost *feel* her catching up to him.

Thank God the light was very much real, and he had to blink a couple of times when they first hit his eyes: LED lightbulbs from the other side of a pair of windows facing a wide-open front yard.

He staggered toward the brightness, like a dying patient toward "the light." Except this one wasn't going to lead him "up there," but rather "down there." More than a dozen women, over the course of a ten-year career, had made damned sure of that.

As he got closer, he was able to make out the square shape of a log cabin, wider than it was tall, with a front porch. There was a white minivan parked out front. The yard hadn't been tended to in a long time, which meant this was some kind of summer retreat. This area of the country was filled with hunters, some of who didn't really follow hunting season rules.

He braced against one of the trees for a moment to look the property over.

A dirt road led to the front door of the cabin, where he could see silhouetted shapes moving across one of the living room windows. That would explain the voices he could just barely hear coming from inside—

Snap! from behind him again.

Still far away, but she was getting closer.

He pushed off and stumbled out of the tree line and toward the cabin.

The minivan had out-of-state plates, which was a good sign. Out-of-towners might not know about the things he had done, regardless of how much time had passed since the last time he had been in the news. The windows were tinted so he couldn't see inside the vehicle, and when he tried the driver-side door, it wouldn't budge. The passenger side and side hatch also wouldn't move when he pulled at them.

He smirked. Of course it was too much to hope for a getaway car with a key still in the ignition. Then again, he had always been the optimistic type, so why stop now?

He turned his attention to the cabin instead.

Halfway to the front door, he unzipped his black jacket to expose the khaki-colored shirt and black tie underneath. He didn't bother fixing his hair or wiping the sweat and traces of blood off his face. All of that would add to the sales pitch he had coming up.

He climbed the three steps up the porch, each one flimsier than the last. Rotten wood, no doubt from lack of maintenance, creaked under him. The state of the cabin's exterior didn't look like anyone regularly visited this place, which meant he was definitely dealing with out-of-towners. Even better if they were kids taking the old man's (or uncle's) cabin for a spin.

Voices floated through the cracks in the doorframe and windows as he neared.

Definitely young people. Maybe early twenties.

He suddenly remembered the knife in his hand and paused to slip it back into its nylon sheath strapped to his left hip. He took a breath before knocking once on the door, then glancing over his shoulder to make sure she hadn't caught up to him yet, turned around and knocked a second time.

How many minutes did he have on her? One? Two? Five? Maybe just seconds—

The door opened and a young woman—blonde and green-eyed, with marvelous legs under white shorts despite the chilly evening—peered out at him from the partial opening. She had smartly kept the chain in place, but he could see enough of her to know she was definitely his type.

Twice in one day. This must be my lucky night.

"Jesus," she said before turning and shouting, "Wade! There's a guy here, and he's bleeding all over your porch!"

He couldn't help but grin to himself. The girl had a way of getting right to the point.

A twenty-something man with short brown hair *(Wade, I presume)* appeared promptly behind the blonde and peered out at him. "Holy shit, man, you okay?"

"No," he said. "I'm definitely not okay."

Then he casually brushed the sides of his jacket back to reveal the perfectly round emblem with a silver star in the middle.

"You a cop?" Wade asked, staring at the badge pinned to his shirt.

Captain Obvious, this kid.

"My name's Beckard," he said. "I'm a state trooper, and I need your help. There's a crazy woman with a shotgun right behind me."

CHAPTER 5

THE TRAIL OF blood led her all the way to a clearing, but even before she reached the edge, she could already see the bright LED lights filtering through the line of trees. She instinctively clicked off the flashlight duct taped to the barrel of the shotgun so it wouldn't give away her position.

A minivan sat in the front yard of a log cabin. There were two windows, both splashed with bright lights, and she could make out figures moving on the other side of one of them. She traced the blood to the minivan, where, judging by the circling pattern of the drips, she guessed he was hoping to find a way into the vehicle. Not finding one, he had decided to go to the cabin instead.

A cabin meant people—even all the way out here, far from the highway—and she didn't need people right now. She had hoped to have a full night to hunt him down and finish it, but that wasn't going to happen now.

So stop bitching about it and adapt. You trained for this, remember?

She darted out of the woods and to the side of the van, keeping as low as possible to avoid detection. The black clothes helped, and though she had tied her hair in a ponytail, it was still blonde, which made it stand out in the darkness.

The side of the minivan was cold against her back even through the sweater and T-shirt underneath. She moved alongside it and peered into a back window but couldn't make out very much through the tinted glass. If he hadn't seen anything worthwhile in there, it was doubtful there would be anything for her to find, so she moved on to the cabin just as he had...how long ago? How much of a head start did he have on her?

At least ten minutes, maybe more...

She heard voices and moved quickly to the side of the closest window.

There was definitely more than one voice, which meant he wasn't the only one inside the cabin. Which made sense. Someone had to have come in the minivan.

So how many? That was the question. How many civilians did she have to deal with? And how would they react to a woman in black barging in on them with a loaded shotgun?

Can't be helped. Gotta finish it tonight.

First, she stood quietly in the darkness and listened.

At least two men, including him, along with a woman's voice. Maybe a girl. Young.

She moved closer to the window and peered in from the side.

Sonofabitch.

He was inside, all right, and he was wearing a state trooper's uniform. Just the khaki shirt and brown pants. The shirt was partially unbuttoned, the tail pulled out of the waistline, and he was sitting in a chair as a young brunette tended to him. Another woman, a blonde, stood next to a young man with brown hair and watched. They all looked in their early twenties, which made *him* stand out even more.

He was grimacing as the brunette dabbed at the buckshot wounds in his side. She was treating it with some kind of ointment before taking a roll of gauze tape and wrapping it around his waist. The girl seemed to know what she was doing. It was just her luck he would stumble into the arms of a paramedic. Or a medical student. Something medical-related, probably.

She pulled back and stood against the wall, gathering herself. She could feel the heat from inside pulsating through her sweater.

What to do, what to do?

She was so close. And he was injured; a wounded animal. All that was left was to go inside and finish him off. Put him out of his misery. It was the humane thing to do. Civilization would thank her for it.

So go do it already.

She unclutched and clutched the Remington.

It would be easy. She had the weapon. What would three twenty-something kids do against that? Nothing. Not a goddamn thing. She could try to convince them, but that might prove fruitless. She would have to spin one hell of a story, and there was too much background to fill them in on. It would take all night.

And she didn't have all night.

She had *one* night.

No. She didn't have time for that. She had come this far, gotten this close, and—

Goddammit.

She pushed off the wall and bent over as she moved across the window, staying under the windowsill. She made it to the other side unseen (or, at least, she hoped she had) and walked straight up the rest of the way. Instead of going around the porch and using the steps, she climbed up from the side. The door wasn't far away from the edge, but the wooden planks creaked loudly under her as she tiptoed across them.

The door had a lever with a hasp lock, probably for the owners to lock the place up when the cabin wasn't in use. She gripped the metal lever and twisted. It moved slightly and without resistance.

She let go and took a step back, then sucked in a deep gulp of the chilly night air.

He's in there. Go get him.

She gripped the lever again with her left hand, her right holding the shotgun at her side.

Finish it.

Finish it!

On the third deep breath, she yanked the lever down and the door moved out of its frame. She pushed it forward as hard as she could—*and it snapped against a chain on the other side and refused to open any further!*

No, no, no!

Alarm bells flooded her senses and she took a quick step back, angled her left shoulder against the door, and threw her entire body into it. The chain snapped and went *clink-clink-clink* as pieces of it sprinkled across the floorboards.

The door swung open in a wide arc and she stumbled inside, losing her balance temporarily. Got control, raised the shotgun, and reached for the forend with her left hand. Got a firm grip and spun to her right, where the four people were gathered in the living room in front of a fireplace that hadn't been lit in God knew how long.

Wide-eyed, they stared back at her. The two girls and their male friend, and *him,* still seated in the chair with one hand over his bandaged side and the other reaching for a knife in its sheath against his left hip.

She smiled at him.

Got you, motherfucker.

She started to pull the trigger when she realized one of the girls—the brunette who had dressed his wounds—was standing too close, and if she fired now—

"Get the fuck away from him!" she shouted.

The brunette didn't get the fuck away from him. She stood frozen in place, paralyzed with fear, that deer in the headlights look the only thing keeping her from being ripped apart by buckshot at any second.

A loud *thump!* drew her attention, and she swung the shotgun over at the blonde, who had dropped a plastic first aid kit box from her numbed fingers. The young man slid protectively in front of her, throwing up his arms as if that was going to stop the Remington. "Don't shoot!" he shouted.

"Get the hell away—" she started to say, when blinding pain exploded through her body as something—a tank, maybe—smashed into her from behind, knocking her forward.

Knocked forward? No. More like *tossed* forward.

She landed on the dirt-caked floor about the same time the shotgun, jostled from her hands by the blow, *clattered* a few yards from her outstretched fingers. It kept skidding until it bumped up against the point of a steel-toe boot, where it rested. Her back screamed as if the spine had been snapped. She had landed on her stomach and one side of her face, and the pain was excruciating, though she couldn't tell which hurt more—her stomach or face or, more likely, her back. But all of that was nothing against the voice screaming inside her head, telling her to *Get up! Get up now, before it's too late! You're too close! Don't let him get away!*

But she couldn't get up because something heavy had fallen on top of her, and it took her a moment to realize it was a man sitting down on her back. Large, strong hands grabbed her arms and twisted them backward, and she became aware of someone screaming.

Her. She was screaming.

Because the man was pinning her arms back in a way that the angle was all wrong, and she was certain both arms would snap at any second.

"Stop it!" someone shouted. One of the young women. "You're hurting her!"

"That's the point, Sabrina!" a male voice said. It was coming from the heavy thing sitting on her back. "Someone grab that shotgun!"

"I got it," another male voice said.

No. No, not him. Not him.

She managed to lift her head despite every inch of her body protesting just in time to see the state trooper bending and picking the Remington up from the floor. He held the shotgun and looked down at her, meeting her stare. Her eyes dropped a bit to the nametag over his right breast pocket: "Beckard."

There was a glint in his eyes—the same brown eyes from

earlier in the woods when he was convinced he was the hunter and she the prey. Then, the corners of his lips began to curve slowly until they formed a smile. It was on the sly and meant only for her. And just like that it was gone, before the others in the cabin could see it.

"Thank you, guys," he said. "You just saved my life."

CHAPTER 6

WELL, SHIT, THIS worked out pretty well.

He had to summon every ounce of willpower just to keep from grinning from ear to ear for longer than half a second at a time. It was hard. Even more difficult to keep the laughter from bursting out of him. Definitely one of those LMAO moments. Or maybe even a LMFBO.

Because this was funny. This was so goddamned funny.

"Is this her?" the brunette who had patched him up asked. She was staring at the woman as the big jock continued to hold her down. "She doesn't look dangerous."

"Trust me, she's dangerous," he said, turning the Remington over in his hands.

"Is that yours?" Wade asked, nodding at the weapon.

The kid (well, he was a kid to Beckard, anyway) stood protectively over his girlfriend, Rachel, while one eye remained fixed on the woman struggling on the floor. The big kid, Donnie, had her pinned in some kind of wrestling move. He had at least a solid hundred pounds on her and had both of her arms wrenched back. It looked painful.

"He's dangerous!" the woman shouted, her eyes darting to

everyone in the cabin except him. "You don't know what you're doing! He's going to kill all of you!"

"You're the one with the shotgun," Rachel said, leaning around Wade just far enough to get a good look at the woman.

"He's a killer!"

"Shut up," Donnie said and put more pressure on her arms, making her cry out.

"Donnie, stop it," the brunette said, walking over. She was a small thing, and too skinny. Definitely not Beckard's type. "You're hurting her."

"I would stop if she didn't keep trying to get up," Donnie said.

"Just go easy, okay?"

The big guy nodded and relaxed his grip a bit on the woman's arms. "Better?"

"Yes," the girl said. She crouched in front of the woman and gave her an almost apologetic look. "Please stop struggling. You're only hurting yourself."

"He's dangerous," the woman said through clenched teeth. She was focusing on Sabrina, obviously having decided that was where her salvation lay. "He's not who you think he is."

"He's a cop," Donnie said.

"He's a killer!"

"You're the one who kicked in our door with a shotgun," Rachel said. She had emerged out from behind Wade's protective force field, apparently having decided it was safe again.

"I had no choice!"

Beckard almost felt sorry for her. He could see the strained expression on her face, a mixture of pain and irritation. Maybe mostly pain. She looked past Sabrina and glared at him, and

Beckard, again, had to summon all his willpower not to grin mischievously back at her. He was close, so close, but he could feel Wade watching him and managed to rein it in.

"You still have that cell phone?" he asked Wade instead.

The twenty-something nodded and turned to his girlfriend. "Babe, go get it for him, will you?"

Rachel hurried off, disappearing into a hallway in the back. The bedroom was back there, Beckard guessed. He made a mental note of that for later.

"How's the reception?" he asked Wade.

"Spotty," Wade said, "but we've been able to connect every time we've tried since we got here."

"Good to hear." He let his eyes dramatically fall back to the woman squirming on the floor when he added, "I need to call for some backup. She's a lot more dangerous than she looks." He touched his bandaged side for effect. "I didn't see it coming at all. One minute she's in the back of my squad car, the next she's gotten the handcuffs off."

"How did she get your shotgun?" Donnie asked.

The woman had stopped struggling against Donnie, probably realizing she wasn't going to get free. She was now listening, glancing from Sabrina to Wade and back to him. He could practically imagine her mind turning, processing, trying to get a grip on the situation. He couldn't help but be impressed with her attitude.

We could so make beautiful music together...

...if only she'd stop trying to kill me.

"I wish I knew," Beckard said. He let out a disappointed sigh. "I don't even know how she got out of those cuffs. I'm just lucky she didn't finish the job and that I found you guys first."

"She took your gun belt, too?" Wade asked.

"Yeah. I was unconscious for a while after we crashed." He shook his head. "She's a lot tougher than she looks," he said, directing that at Donnie. "You should be really careful with her."

"She's not going anywhere," Donnie said. "I can sit on her all night if I have to."

"Hopefully you won't have to."

Rachel came out of the back with a cell phone and handed it to him. He noticed her hand was still shaking slightly even though she was putting on a brave face.

"Thanks, Rachel," he said. Then, with as much concern as he could muster, "You okay?"

She shook her head, and he decided he liked the way her long blonde hair flitted from side to side when she did that. "I'm just really freaked right now, that's all. I'll be fine."

"You're doing great, babe," Wade said. He held out his hand and Rachel walked over, took it, and slipped back into his protective force field.

Ah, must be true love, Beckard thought. "Don't worry, I'll get her out of your hair soon and you guys can go back to enjoying your vacation." He smiled at Rachel. "You'll be all right, I promise."

She gave him a half-smile back and Beckard thought, *Damn, I poured that on pretty thick. Hopefully I didn't scare her off.*

"Got any bars?" Wade asked him.

He nodded. "Plenty," he said, walking to one of the windows and pretending to look out while he dialed a number on the phone.

He glanced over his shoulder at the woman, catching her defiant glare. He was surprised she had given up trying to convince the kids. Then again, she was smart and probably figured out she had no chance of success. Or very little. After all, he was a pretty damn good liar and held all the cards. And now he had the shotgun, too.

The kids were milling about as he dialed, but he caught the small brunette watching him curiously, almost suspiciously.

She's gonna be a problem, that one.

Someone finally picked up on the other end of the phone call, the voice coming through the speaker placed against his ear where only he could hear it. "The number you have dialed is no longer in service," a computerized female voice answered. "Please hang up and try again."

Beckard ignored the voice and said into the phone, "Hey, Diane, it's me." He paused briefly before continuing. "Yeah, tell the captain I ran into some trouble escorting that woman back to the station. We got into a car accident and she escaped." Another dramatic pause, followed by, "I almost died but I'm okay, thanks to some kids at a cabin in the woods." He threw a quick look back at Wade. "What's the address here?"

Wade told him, and he repeated it into the phone.

"...please hang up and try again," the computerized voice repeated for the fourth time.

"Yeah, as soon as you can," he said into the phone, then wiped at a string of dirty sweat on his forehead. "Great, thanks Diane. I'll wait for them here." He ended the call, walked over, and handed the phone back to Rachel. "Thanks for letting me borrow it."

She nodded and put the phone away with one hand, the other still wrapped tightly around Wade's waist.

"What'd they say?" Sabrina asked.

"They're sending two squad cars over to take us back," he said before glancing down at his watch. "I guess two hours?"

"That's a long time," Wade said.

"The station's about twenty miles up the highway, and they're going to have to look for this place. I'm just glad they had enough people on the night shift to come get us. We're usually pretty low on manpower after sundown." He looked at the woman. She was still staring daggers at him from the floor. "She's dangerous, guys. We have to be really careful with her."

"Don't sweat it," Donnie said. "You got your shotgun back, and I'm sitting on her. What's she gonna do?"

Beckard smiled. "Good point, Donnie."

"What now?" Wade asked.

"Sit back and wait for my reinforcements to arrive. Then we'll be out of your hair, and you guys can all pretend tonight never happened." He touched his side for effect again. "Well, it'll be a while yet for me, but it's all part of the job, I guess."

"Hey, Donnie, we packed that duct tape, right?" Wade asked.

Donnie thought about it, then nodded. "Back in the van, in my bag. Why?"

"So we can tie her up, since—" he turned to Beckard "—you don't have your cuffs anymore, right?"

He shook his head. "I don't know what she did with them. Probably threw them into the woods."

"He's *lying*," the woman said. "Don't believe anything he says. He's a killer!"

"Who?" the brunette asked.

"Him!" she shouted, staring at Beckard. "He's dangerous!"

Beckard ignored her and said to Wade, "Can you go get that

duct tape?"

"Sure," Wade said. Then, he added, looking over at the woman, "Maybe we can use it to shut her up, too."

"Sounds like a plan," Beckard grinned back at him.

CHAPTER 7

TEN YEARS OF research, six years of training, and three years of getting ready for this moment…and this is how it ends. Sitting on the floor of a cabin in the woods, bound and helpless. It wasn't even close to what she had imagined during all those lonely nights lying in bed alone trying to picture every scenario in her head; all the things that could go wrong and all the twists and turns that had to be accounted for. She had it all figured out.

Or thought she did, anyway.

And the night had started off so promising, too.

"What's your name?" the small brunette asked her.

"Allie," she said.

"What did you do, Allie?"

"I didn't do anything," she said, looking back at the girl who had just patched up the man she had spent the last ten years of her life trying to find, and having found, had just failed to kill.

It's not over yet. You can still salvage this.

She leaned slightly forward, toward the girl. "He's lying."

"About what?" the girl, Sabrina, asked.

Not really a girl. A young woman. Twenty? Twenty-one? Young enough to be on break from college and old enough to actually be in college. The last time Allie was on a school campus, that was when—

No! Concentrate on the present!

There's still a chance to save this!

They had sat her in one corner of the cabin with her wrists and ankles bound with duct tape they had retrieved from the van outside. The restraints cut off most of her ability to move and drove home her dire situation.

Ten years of research…

They had wanted to cover up her mouth to keep her quiet, too, but Sabrina argued in her favor. For some reason they listened to the girl, even the two big guys. Donnie, the jackass who had tackled her from behind and then sat down on her, and Wade, the tall lanky one with the blonde girlfriend.

"Allie," Sabrina said, directing Allie's attention back to her small round face. "You said he was lying. What's he lying about?"

"About everything. Don't believe anything he says. Every word that comes out of his mouth is a lie."

She was in the living room with Sabrina, with Donnie in the kitchen to her right pulling meat cuts from a cooler and preparing a portable skillet. Donnie seemed disinterested in their conversation, as if none of the last hour was in any way out of the ordinary for him. Wade and Rachel had gone into one of the bedrooms in the back, while Beckard was in the bathroom "cleaning up." He had been gone for two minutes, but soon he'd be back.

She focused on Sabrina. "He's not who he claims to be."

"Beckard?" Sabrina said.

"Yes."

"Who is he?"

"He's a killer."

"You mean because he's killed someone in the line of duty?"

"No. Because he's a *killer*."

Sabrina looked confused. "I don't understand."

"He's not a cop." She shook her head. "At least, I don't think he is."

"You don't think he is?" Again, that look of confusion. Maybe a little suspicion had even slipped in there.

No, no, I'm losing her...

She struggled for the right words, but they were elusive. "In all the research I've done, nothing ever pointed to him being a cop."

"Research? On Beckard?"

"He's a maniac. Have you ever heard of the Roadside Killer?"

"No..."

"No?"

Sabrina shook her head. "We're not from around here. This cabin belongs to Wade's uncle."

"The Roadside Killer is a serial killer," Allie said.

She tried to sound as calm as possible, even though her back still throbbed from being hit and sat on, and her legs and arms were already going numb from the restraints. The last thing she wanted was to look like a crazy woman in front of the only person who could be of any use to her. She couldn't rely on Donnie—the kid seemed lost in his own world, arranging meat on the skillet. And Rachel and Wade had bought Beckard's story wholesale.

So she had this little girl. This brunette, who looked so much like—

No. Concentrate!

"Seven years ago, he was all over the news," Allie said. "He killed six people that the authorities are sure of. Even more that they don't have a clue about."

"The Roadside Killer?" Sabrina repeated.

"Yes. You've never heard of him? Never?"

She shook her head again. "Sorry. You said seven years ago?"

"Since the last time the authorities heard of him, yes."

"I was a freshman in high school seven years ago, but I still never heard of the Roadside Killer."

"What's she saying?" Donnie asked from the kitchen.

Sabrina glanced over. "She says the state trooper's a serial killer called the Roadside Killer. You ever heard of him?"

Donnie didn't even think about it. "Nope. She crazy or what?"

Sabrina looked back. "I don't know. Maybe..."

"I'm not crazy," Allie said. She could feel her patience slipping and prayed it didn't show on her face. "I'm telling you the truth."

"That's what makes someone crazy. They actually believe what they're saying. It's part of the psychosis."

Sabrina stood up.

"Wait," Allie said.

"I'm sorry," the girl said. "I hope you get some help."

"Sabrina—"

But Sabrina ignored her and walked over to the kitchen and began talking to Donnie in a soft voice. The big man smiled and they kissed briefly before going back to getting the food ready.

And just like that, her opportunity was gone.

Allie sighed, leaned her head back against the wall, and tried to regroup.

Of course the girl didn't believe her. She had burst into their cabin with a shotgun, chasing a state trooper whom she had already tried to kill and left a bloody mess. She couldn't imagine what her face must have looked like at the time. Wild, eyes bloodshot—it probably wasn't a very pretty sight.

I don't blame them...

She watched Donnie putting large chunks of rib eye onto the skillet. The smell of meat cooking instantly filled the cabin. Her stomach growled despite the fact she had eaten less than four hours ago back at the diner. That was where she was sure he had spotted her and followed her onto the road—

He came out of the bathroom with his shirt untucked, the fabric still covered in patches of blood he couldn't wash off. He was wiping his hands on a paper napkin, the shotgun tucked under one armpit. She saw his eyes checking the living room as soon as he stepped out of the hallway. They picked her up first before snapping over to the kitchen, then back to her. He was reading the scene, trying to decide if everything was the way he had left it.

When he sneaked a smile in her direction, she knew he was convinced (rightly) that he still had the upper hand. She wished she could have said he was wrong.

"That smells good," he said to Donnie and Sabrina. "You guys came prepared."

"We have enough for one more," Sabrina said. "You're welcome to join us until the other troopers show up."

"I've never turned down a free steak before."

He smiled easily and got a return smile from Sabrina.

Hook, line, and sinker.

He's done this before. Conned his way out of a jam.

Of course he has. He's been doing this for ten years now…

He walked past her without giving her a second look, as if he had forgotten she existed at all. He sat down gingerly on one of the stools next to Sabrina, making a show of grimacing for the couple's benefit.

"You okay?" Sabrina asked.

He gave her a manufactured I'm-gritting-it-out attempt at a smile. "Just an hour and change before my boys get here. I'll be fine."

"Maybe we should take you to a hospital first. I mean, you were just shot."

"It hurts like hell, I'm not going to lie, but it's not life threatening. I guess she's not the world's best shot."

"You've been shot before?" Donnie asked.

"First time."

"Hurts?"

"Oh yeah," he said, and they both chuckled.

"What did she do, anyway?" Sabrina asked, looking back at Allie.

Beckard did, too. "Her boyfriend went missing a few months ago. She's a person of interest."

"Whacked her boyfriend?" Donnie said, then whistled. "Talk about a rough breakup."

"Donnie," Sabrina said, rolling her eyes.

The big blond laughed. "Too soon?"

Sabrina ignored him and said to Beckard, "Have you figured out how she got out of your handcuffs yet?"

"Not a clue," Beckard said. "I didn't even know she was that dangerous. The captain just asked me to bring her into the station for questioning. I guess you never know what a person is capable of until they reveal their true colors."

God, he's good at this.

But she had to remind herself that he had ten years of practice. He had been lying his way through dozens of bodies, six that the authorities—the *real* authorities—knew about, and even more they wouldn't admit was his handiwork.

"How's Rachel doing?" Beckard asked.

"She's still a little freaked out, but she'll be fine," Sabrina said. "Wade's with her now."

"They're involved?"

"They've been dating since high school."

"Well, it's good she has him," Beckard said. "It can be pretty traumatizing when guns and crazy people are involved."

"Yeah, they're really good together." Then she said to Donnie, "Got an ETA on those steaks, chief?"

"Ten minutes," Donnie said. "Well done, right?"

"Of course."

"What about you?" he asked Beckard.

"Medium rare," Beckard said. "I like a little blood on the plate."

"Shit, me too," the big twenty-something said, and they both chuckled again.

"Make sure mine's really well done," Sabrina said.

"Yeah, yeah," Donnie said.

"Make sure they're well done this time, Donnie."

"I said okay, didn't I?"

"That's what you said last time."

"Nag nag nag."

The two young people were bickering about the steak, allowing Beckard to sneak a glance back across the cabin. Except he wasn't looking at Allie, but all the way to the hallway in the back and the bedrooms on the other end. Wade was comforting Rachel in one of those rooms at the moment.

Rachel...

Tall. Blonde. And pretty.

How had she missed it? The girl was exactly Beckard's type.

Just like she had made herself into, in order to draw him in.

Just like Carmen had been ten years ago...

CHAPTER 8

AN HOUR AND a half. He had that long to make it happen. The problem was the other three people in the cabin with Rachel. He'd have to get rid of them first before his "reinforcements" were supposed to show up.

The short girl, Sabrina, didn't look all that athletic, and while he saw intelligence between those brown eyes, it took more than brains to stop him. The big guy, Donnie, would definitely be a problem. But Donnie was stupid, so maybe he was giving the kid too much credit. The other guy, Wade, didn't look any smarter, but two meatheads were still one more than he liked to deal with at the same time.

And then, of course, there was the woman.

Allie.

That could be a made up name. Who knew what kind of lies she was telling the kids to get them on her side? She had already proven pretty damn resourceful, so he wouldn't put it past her to be just as creative when it came to spinning a tale on the fly. If Beckard was good at one thing, it was hearing opportunity when it knocked, and he'd be goddamned if it wasn't knocking pretty loudly at the moment.

Fortunately for him, the woman was tied up with duct tape and hadn't moved from the corner where she sat quietly, head bent down in defeat. He didn't believe it for a second. She was listening, absorbing everything he was telling the others and trying to figure out an alternative plan of action. Because she was smart and she knew she didn't have a chance of convincing them he was the bad guy, not after kicking in their door with a shotgun.

That was so dramatic, too. Like a heroine in an action movie.

Ha!

He might have chuckled out loud, because Sabrina glanced over. "You say something?"

"I'm not sure, but I think the wound might have opened up," he said, looking down at his side. "It feels like it's burning. Can you take a look?"

Sabrina climbed off her stool. "Come on, the first aid kit's in the bathroom, and I can clean some of that blood off for you."

He got off the stool and reached for the shotgun on the counter—

"You don't need that," Sabrina said.

He pulled his hand back and smiled at her before saying to Donnie, "Keep an eye on it for me, will ya?"

The big kid nodded. "Meat'll be done by the time you guys get back." He turned one of the rib eye steaks over on the portable grill and grinned happily. "Can I cook or can I cook?"

"Just don't burn mine again, Emeril Lagasse," Sabrina said. Then to Beckard, "Come on, let's get you fixed up."

Beckard got off his stool and followed the brunette across the cabin.

As he walked past her, he glanced at Allie. Her head remained lowered, eyes staring at the floor as if she had withdrawn into her own world.

Bullshit.

He kept watching her, and just as he had almost passed her, she peeked and they locked eyes.

I knew it.

He winked, then stepped into the hallway after Sabrina.

IT WAS GOING to be tricky with the big one outside and the couple in the room just down the hall from him at this very moment. He had to be very quiet, but at the same time very efficient. Fortunately, he had a lot of experience at doing both.

"She believes it," the girl was saying.

"What's that?"

"What she's saying about you." As she said that last part, she sneaked a look at him, as if trying to gauge his reaction. "She really does think you're this serial killer they called the Roadside Killer. Why would she think that?"

"I guess she's more mentally disturbed than I thought." He feigned sadness. "I've seen a lot of crazy things in this job, but what happened tonight...I didn't think she was capable of something like that."

"Even after what she did to her boyfriend?"

"We don't really know what she did to him, if anything."

"Innocent until proven guilty?" Sabrina said, smiling at him as if to say, *"You poor boy, you still believe in that silliness?"*

He shrugged. "She was just a person of interest. I didn't see any of this coming at all."

"Still, she must have been pretty strong to knock you out. She doesn't look that strong."

"She had a little help. I hit my forehead on the steering wheel after the car went spinning off the road."

"How did she manage that?"

He didn't answer right away. Sabrina was unwinding the gauze around his waist to get a look at the wound underneath, but he noticed how she kept sneaking a look at his face by employing a variety of methods and angles, including using the dirt-stained mirror to their right to watch his reflection. She probably thought he didn't know, but he knew.

Smart little bitch.

Not smart enough.

"I don't know," he said finally. "Man, the guys are going to have a field day at my expense when they hear about this, I can tell you that."

"I can imagine. Guys being guys, I mean."

"It's worse with cops."

"You don't know where she put your gun belt?"

"No idea. She probably tossed it or something. She already had the shotgun. I was lucky to get out of there alive."

"Maybe someone already found your car."

"I don't think so. When I came to, we were pretty deep in the woods. I must have stepped on the gas after she hit me from behind for us to get that far off the highway."

Goddamn, I'm good at this. Who knew?

Sabrina tossed the bloody strips into a trash bin and peered at the wound for a moment. "Well, it's not too bad. It's mostly stopped bleeding. Does it still hurt?"

"More like nonstop tingling."

"You were shot, so I'm guessing you'll be tingling for a while. It looks like you'll be okay until someone smarter than me and with a lot more medical school education looks at you."

"You're doing a pretty good job."

She smiled almost shyly. "Thanks. I guess when you get right down to it, humans are basically animals who haven't learned how to walk on all fours yet."

He grinned and didn't try to stop it that time because he figured it was the right reaction in response to a joke she probably had on standby. "Glad I stumbled into a veterinarian student all the way out here."

"Must be your lucky night."

"I'd say so. Aside from the whole getting shot part, I mean."

She chuckled. "Still, you're doing pretty good."

"Yeah, I guess so."

She turned back to the first aid kit sitting on the counter and opened it. "Sit back."

He did and let her roll another fresh strip of gauze around his waist. He could do a lot of things, but fixing his own wounds so he wouldn't bleed to death wasn't one of them. He blamed it on all the success he'd had over the years. Until now, until tonight, it had all been smooth sailing.

Then Allie showed up.

Christ, she lured me right in. The woman is cold as ice.

We could so make beautiful music together.

"I know about Wade and Rachel," he said, "but you and Donnie?"

"We're getting there," Sabrina said, again with that slightly shy half-smile.

"Does he play football or something?"

"Donnie? Nah. He's just a big Neanderthal."

Beckard chuckled. "He's a pretty big kid. That size's going to waste."

"He played in high school, but he was never good enough to get a scholarship or anything. I like him anyway, his primitive DNA and all." When she was done, she put the rest of the roll back into the plastic white box. "You should try not to move too much until your friends get you to an actual doctor."

"I wish I could do that, but I have too many things going on right now."

"Like what?"

"You, for instance."

She might have looked confused, but her back was to him and he couldn't verify her reaction. "Me?"

"Yeah, you. Donnie and Wade, too. You guys are in my way."

"I don't understand," she said, turning around. "In your way how—"

She never got a chance to finish, because he had already sank the first three inches of the knife into her side, and as she opened her mouth to gasp—or perhaps to scream—he clasped his left hand over it.

He pushed her back up against the counter and shoved in the remaining seven inches of steel. Her eyes widened into giant saucers, so wide that he imagined them popping and shooting across the room, maybe even bouncing off the closed door behind him and going *splat* against the floor, like in a cartoon.

Instead, she slumped against the counter, and he grabbed her around the waist and guided her body slowly to the floor. With the knife still embedded in her side, there wasn't a lot of blood. Only a thin trickle managed to drip out of the wound and along the black handle, speckling the dirty tile floor.

Beckard took his hand away from her mouth only after she had stopped moving completely. He craned his head and listened for noises but could only smell sizzling steaks wafting into the room under the slot in the door.

He turned back to Sabrina, then pulled the knife gently out of her side to avoid the splashing effect. He wiped the blade on her shirt, then put it back into its nylon sheath before standing up and checking himself in the mirror.

Satisfied he didn't have any extra *(fresh)* blood on him, Beckard flicked off the lights, then opened the bathroom door.

He felt like whistling but managed to stop himself just in time. He was giddy, which was something he didn't have to temper because it didn't really show outwardly. Or, at least, he didn't think it did.

One down and two to go before he could start having fun again...

CHAPTER 9

SHE'S DEAD. THE girl's dead.

The thought raced through her head the instant Beckard reappeared out of the hallway by himself. When she saw his face—and that glib expression plastered all over it—she had no doubts whatsoever.

The girl was dead. Sabrina. Who had the kind of intense gaze and intelligent eyes that reminded her so much of her—

Stop it! Concentrate on the moment!

"Donnie!" Allie shouted.

Donnie was moving one of the steaks over to a plate when he glanced up. "What?"

"She's dead! Sabrina's dead!"

"What the fuck you talking about?"

Beckard paused briefly and looked at her, and she could tell she had caught him off guard.

"She's dead!" Allie shouted. "Inside the bathroom, Donnie! He killed Sabrina when they were in the bathroom!"

Donnie looked across the cabin at Beckard. "What's she talking about? Where's Sabrina?"

"She's finishing up," Beckard said as he resumed his walk

across the cabin living room.

She was amazed at how casual he was, as if he were on a Sunday stroll instead of having just left a body behind in the bathroom. She had expected a bigger reaction from him— something, *anything* to give away that he was flustered by her accusation.

"She'll be out soon," Beckard said.

"Don't trust him," Allie said. "He's lying, Donnie. Sabrina's in there, and she's dead. He killed her."

Donnie glanced at her again, then back at Beckard, like a child caught between two bickering parents, unable to decide who to trust. The big metal fork was still clutched in his hand, and she tried to will him to stick it into Beckard's gut.

"Why is she saying that?" Donnie asked.

"She's crazy; don't listen to her," Beckard said. He was halfway across the living room now, and passing her. "She knows she's going to jail after this. She's just desperate."

"Don't listen to him!" Allie shouted. "Sabrina's in there! He killed her with that knife!"

Donnie's eyes shifted to the knife on Beckard's hip. She wondered if there was still blood on the blade. Maybe if she could get Donnie to look at it—

Beckard had detoured at the last second and crouched in front of her. "Give it a rest. No one's going to believe a crazy woman."

Allie ignored him and focused on Donnie instead. "Don't let him get the shotgun, Donnie! Make him take you to the bathroom! You'll see—"

Beckard had picked up the roll of duct tape from the floor when she wasn't looking, and he slapped a strip over her mouth now, cutting off the rest of her warning. She tried to get up but lost her balance and fell back down, landing sideways on the floor.

Beckard stood back up. "Don't listen to her, Donnie. She's crazy, remember? She'll say anything to get out of this. I wouldn't be surprised if we find out she really did do something to her boyfriend."

Allie managed to turn herself until she could see Donnie in the kitchen. He had picked up the shotgun and was holding it at his side as he walked around the counter.

Thank God he's smarter than he looks.

"But what's she saying, about Sabrina?" Donnie said. "Where is she?"

"I told you, she's in the bathroom, cleaning up," Beckard said. "It's my fault. I was bleeding, and I guess I made a mess."

The man's voice was amazingly relaxed, even...*soothing*. Was this how he had lured all his victims, she wondered. This unnatural calmness, even when confronted with a frazzled boyfriend holding a shotgun? Was this what allowed him to get away with it all these years? This sociopathic personality, this uncanny ability to spin lies at a moment's notice?

In all the research she had done on Beckard (even though she never knew his name until now), one thing was always certain: He was smart. Or maybe the right word was cunning. And now she could add creative to that list. The man simply knew how to adapt and overcome. It was an amazingly impressive trait, something to be admired if he was anything other than a sick murderer piece of shit.

"You can go and check for yourself," Beckard was saying. "I swear, Donnie, I didn't do anything. You can't listen to her.

Remember what she did? She almost shot Sabrina with that shotgun earlier. And she might have, if you hadn't tackled her."

Donnie's eyes snapped back to Allie before returning to Beckard, only to return to her again. She wanted to yell at him to stop looking at her face and focus on Beckard instead, because the state trooper was still walking toward him. Very slowly, each deliberate step getting him closer and closer to Donnie, *to the shotgun.*

Allie tried jerking her head in Beckard's direction to lead his gaze where she wanted it. Tried to scream out the warning with her eyes and frantic head movements, because everything she wanted to say was lost as incoherent mumbling against the duct tape.

Donnie continued to hold the Remington at his side as if it were a third arm he didn't know how to use. Beckard must have seen that, too, because she noticed he had begun moving faster toward the younger man.

"She's inside the bathroom?" Donnie was saying to Beckard. His voice had lost some of its earlier intensity, which made Allie even more desperate. "She's fine?"

"Yeah, of course," Beckard said. "She said she had to clean up because this is Wade's uncle's cabin and she didn't want to leave a mess behind."

That seemed to resonate with Donnie and Allie saw, to her horror, his big body relaxing. "Yeah, she's a stickler for that type of stuff. That's why I love her." Then he put the shotgun back on the counter and Allie's heart sank. "Man, she really got me going there," he said, staring daggers across the room at Allie.

Beckard looked back at her, too. "I guess that's one of her talents. She suckered me in earlier, too. I had no idea what she was capable of until she attacked."

"Girls, man," Donnie said. "Can't live with them…"

"…can't live without them?"

"I was going to say, 'Can't live with them, can't trust them not to bash your head in when you're not looking.'"

They both got a good laugh out of that.

"You're telling me," Beckard said, and rubbed at the back of his head for effect.

"Anyway, steak's ready," Donnie said. "You wanted medium rare, right?"

"Yup. Man, that smells good."

Donnie walked back around the counter and picked up the fork. "She should hurry up. Hers was ready a while ago."

"I don't think she's coming, Donnie," Beckard said.

"Huh?"

"Sabrina. I don't think she's coming out of the bathroom."

Donnie stared at him, confused. "What do you mean?"

Oh, you stupid bastard. You stupid, stupid bastard.

Beckard picked up the shotgun from the counter.

Donnie stared at him, then at the shotgun, before returning his dumbfounded gaze to Beckard. The look on his face said it all. The man didn't quite comprehend what had happened, what was happening, and what would happen in the next few seconds.

"What I mean is, Sabrina's dead," Beckard said. "She's right. I did kill your girlfriend in the bathroom. Sorry, kid."

"You…"

Donnie looked across the room at Allie. She felt sorry for him. Stupid, dumb Donnie.

He turned back to Beckard as the realization sunk in. "You killed her? My Sabrina?"

"Yup," Beckard said, as if he were discussing the weather.

Something burst and Donnie ran around the counter, yelling wildly, raising the fork high above his head to strike. "You fucker!"

Beckard shot him from almost point-blank range and blew a hole through Donnie's chest, the discharge thundering inside the cabin. The big blond twenty-something flopped to the floor, the fork *clattering* a split second before an empty shell flew out of the Remington and landed nearby.

Beckard turned around and shook his head, *tsk tsking* at Allie. "See what you did? I hope you realize this is all your fault."

He hadn't finished talking when loud footsteps filled the room, coming from behind her.

Allie managed to roll around in time to see Wade and Rachel racing out of the hallway. Wade, in front, slid to a stop at the sight of Beckard with the shotgun and Donnie's body half-visible behind the counter.

"What's going on?" Wade asked, his voice trembling.

Instead of answering with his mouth, Beckard chose to let the Remington do it for him. He fired a shot into the ceiling, the second round nearly as deafening as the first.

Rachel, already hidden behind Wade, screamed and pressed her hands against her ears, as if that would magically transport her away from here.

"Donnie's dead, and Sabrina's dead, too," Beckard said. He walked across the room, the barrel of the shotgun pointed at Wade's chest. The weapon, like his hand, was amazingly steady. "Stay calm and don't do anything stupid, and the two of you won't join them. I promise."

Allie frantically tried to catch Wade's eyes.

He's lying, Wade! He's going to kill you and take Rachel!

He's lying! That's what he does! He lies and lies, until he kills you!

Wade didn't seem to even remember she was there as he raised his arms into the air. "Okay, okay, whatever you say, man. Don't hurt us, okay? We'll do whatever you say, just as long as you don't hurt us."

The sound of Beckard's footsteps had stopped, and Allie rolled back around until she bumped up against a familiar steel-toed boot. She looked up at Beckard, who was smiling down at her, the barrel of the shotgun pointing nonchalantly at the ceiling.

The smug look on his face said everything.

He'd won.

Again.

"Two for the price of one," Beckard said. "'Dear Penthouse Forum, I didn't think it would ever happen to me...'"

Then his expression seemed to change and he narrowed his eyes at her. He didn't say anything for a long time and was content to just look at her. This, she realized, was the first time they had stared so closely at one another, and she could see her own reflection in the orbs of his irises.

"You know, you look familiar," he said. "Have we met before?"

CHAPTER 10

"GO TO HELL," she said when he pulled the duct tape off.

Beckard smirked. "That's not very nice. I'm trying to have a conversation with you here."

"Kiss my ass."

"Do you kiss your mom with that mouth?" Before she could answer, he slapped the tape back into place. "Never mind. I think I know what you're going to say." He continued to linger on her face. "I know you, though. I don't know where. Not yet. But I'll figure it out. I always do."

He left her lying on the floor on her side and stood up, then looked over at Wade and Rachel, leaning against each other nearby. Like Allie, their wrists and ankles were bound with duct tape. He had made sure to wrap an extra revolution around Wade just in case the kid proved stronger than he looked. He was tall and gangly and wasn't anywhere close to Donnie's hulking size, but there was no point in taking any chances now.

He lingered on Rachel. She must have sensed him staring, because she turned and pushed herself further against Wade in an attempt to hide herself from him.

Beckard smiled. "Relax; it'll be over soon."

He headed to the kitchen, stepping over Donnie's body. The big kid had bled all over the floor, pieces (well, chunks, anyway) of him still clinging to the countertops, drawers, and cabinets. It was pretty messy, but then Beckard was used to working in and around ugly scenes. He would have liked it to be more orderly, but there was no denying that everything had worked out just great for him, even if he did have to get really creative to keep things going for a while there.

But that was over. Done. Two bodies in the cabin wasn't a big deal. The kids had already told him they weren't expected back at school until Monday. He was, for all intents and purposes, free and clear to do whatever he wanted for forty-eight hours.

Especially with the girl. She was so his type, too.

Beckard sat down on the stool and picked up the fork and knife and cut into the first steak. He was hungry. Starving. There was nothing like almost dying to ramp up the appetite. It was too bad Donnie had overcooked the meat.

Beggars can't be choosers.

He ate by himself, humming quietly between bites.

The woman, Allie, was staring at him from across the room, but he chose to ignore her. Like Rachel, she was his type, too, though he usually preferred them a little more, well, less bloodthirsty.

Still, there was no denying it. The blonde hair, the long legs, the perfect cheekbones…

He made his decision while he was eating. He would take Rachel first, then break Allie later. He might even go against his own rules about spending more than twenty-four hours with each girl. He had a feeling he'd need more than that with Allie.

She might be worth it, too. It had been a while since he'd had this kind of challenge.

That made him remember his aching side. Christ, it hurt. He really should go see a real doctor. He'd have to come up with a good excuse. A hunting accident, maybe. Some idiot in the woods shot him by mistake, then ran off.

Yeah, that might work...

Beckard sensed her still watching him. He looked up and met her eyes and smiled back at her. That made her look away, but he could see the cogs spinning inside her head in the way she glanced around the cabin while pretending she wasn't.

The door, the windows, Wade and Rachel next to her...

Thinking. Evaluating. Adjusting...

He continued to eyeball her over the well-done rib eye.

That face. That side profile.

He knew her from somewhere. He was sure of it, even if he couldn't place her. Not yet, anyway.

He shook his head.

It would come to him.

HE COULDN'T REMEMBER the last time he had eaten so well. God bless him, Donnie had also packed beer in the cooler. Beckard opened one and drained it in two gulps. It would have been a perfect meal if the meat hadn't been so well done that it was practically burnt. Of course, Beckard had to take some blame, too. He had distracted Donnie while the kid was tending to the steaks.

He leaned against the counter, resting on his elbows, and looked across the cabin at the three of them. Wade and Rachel were practically keeping each other upright as they sat on the floor, backs against the wall, which was both romantic and sad. Romantic, in that they clearly had true feelings for one another; sad, in that it wasn't going to do them a bit of good.

Allie had managed to pull herself into a sitting position. She was still looking around the room with calculating eyes, trying not to make it too obvious.

And her face. There was something about her face...

"I know you," he said across the room to her.

She looked over at him, strands of blonde hair falling over her face.

"I know you," he repeated. "I know your face. Allie?" he said, testing the sound of her name against his lips. He shook his head. "I don't know the name, but I know your face. I never forget a face." He let out a loud burp, then grinned. "Pardon me."

He got up and walked around the counter, stepping over Donnie's body a second time, careful to avoid the blood. He left the shotgun behind and crossed over to her with just the beer in one hand. Maybe the alcohol was making him a little cocky, but he'd never felt so in control in his life. He was like a phoenix risen from the ashes. Shotgun ashes. From almost dead to almost winning. Pretty much winning, actually.

He crouched in front of Allie and stared at her face again. Really, really stared this time, from only a few inches away.

He leaned to one side, then the other. Even stood back up to get another angle before crouching again.

She looked back at him the entire time, as if daring him to

do something.

He finally pulled back a bit. "I've seen you before."

He called up the memories, sifting through the faces of all the women from his past. They were like a Rolodex, forever ingrained on his brain. Their names, the various blonde shades, their noses, and the colors of their eyes. The sound of their voices and the way they talked, the way they cried, the way they screamed…

"Maybe not you," he said. "But someone like you." He looked back at the shotgun. "You came prepared."

Nearby, Wade was listening, but Beckard ignored him.

"You wanted me to take you," he continued, zeroing back in on Allie's eyes. "You lured me in. Like a black widow. *'Come into my web, said the spider to the fly.'* And I fell right into it, like a sucker."

He chuckled and took another sip of beer.

"That means you have a grudge. You studied me, didn't you? Not *me*, me. Oh, it's obvious you had no idea who I was. Not my name or what I did for a living. I'm kind of proud of that, actually. It took a lot of effort, you know. A *lot*. But still, you knew the real me. My methods. My modus operandi. The man underneath the façade. You might have even known what I would do, how I would react, in certain situations. The PIT maneuver, for instance. No one's ever managed to escape that. But you did. For two solid miles. You completely threw me off my game with that one. Congratulations."

His legs were getting tired and his side was hurting a bit, so he sat down Indian style in front of her. He placed the beer between them before returning his attention to her.

She continued to watch him back, silently. Not that she had

a choice with the duct tape over her mouth. He thought about removing it, but didn't. She'd just lie or throw some obscenities at him.

"I killed someone close to you, didn't I?" he asked. "Was it a friend? A sister? That's what this is. Revenge."

He saw it—movement in her eyes.

It was small. A tiny flicker, really.

He smiled.

"It was a sister."

He leaned forward some more and once again ran through the Rolodex of all the faces in his head. This time, he used her face as a guide to look for someone else. There were the ones he took in the first three years, before he really knew what he was doing. The dozen or so since that the cops didn't even know about because he had gotten smarter. So, so much smarter. He learned. He adapted. He grew as a killer.

All those women. All those blonde hairs, those blue and green eyes, those long slender legs and perfect cheekbones...

"Carmen," he said.

Another flicker across her face.

Bingo.

"Her name was Carmen," he smiled. "Twenty. She was coming from New York during the holidays. She was all alone out here. I couldn't have asked for an easier target. Heaven sent."

He expected to see her expression crumble with pain and misery now that he had discovered her secret. Instead, air expelled from her flaring nostrils and her entire body tightened up. He could see—even *taste*—her attempts to rein in her emotions, the runaway freight train of anger and fury that was flooding all of her senses right this very second.

He went in for the kill.

"I remember her. She was beautiful. One of the most beautiful women I'd ever seen. Just the loveliest thing on two feet. And my God, she was so much fun. We had a great day together, and she tasted so sweet before, during, and after. I didn't want to let her go, but as they say, all good things must end."

Her eyes burned, threatening to consume him.

He wallowed in her reaction, his grin growing wider.

"In the end I had to throw her back, like all the others. She was beautiful, but she was just another girl. Another victim. Oh, don't get me wrong. She was something. The first time I had her, I practically died with ecstasy—"

She lunged at him, and before Beckard could pull back, his nose exploded and he was toppling backward.

Jesus Christ. It felt like someone had smashed his face in with a sledgehammer.

No, not a sledgehammer. Just her forehead. *Her fucking forehead.*

He didn't know what was happening—the pain was blinding and he might have been screaming—but he wasn't bound and gagged like her, and he managed to stumble up to his feet even as blood poured like a river from his shattered nose.

The cabin's dirty floorboards were covered in blood—*his* blood—and he grabbed at his face with both hands and let out a wild howl that surprised even him.

She was rolling around, trying to get away, and it took him a full second to realize she was going for the shotgun in the kitchen. How the hell she expected to grab it and use it with both hands and ankles bound together with duct tape, and the inability to stand up, was beyond him.

And he didn't care, either.

He stalked her. He thought about coming up with something clever to say. Something punchy *(Ha!)*.

But he couldn't think of anything, and instead he just started kicking her.

First, in the side. She doubled forward from the pain and must have screamed into the duct tape. He kicked her again and felt his boot's steel toe connecting with a ribcage that time. Tears welled up in both her eyes, but he was beyond caring.

He kicked her again, and again, and again.

He didn't stop until she ceased moving completely and his leg was too sore to keep going.

His entire face was burning. *Burning.*

Beckard staggered the short distance to the kitchen and went to the sink. He turned on the faucet and splashed cold water over his face and saw how red the water flowing off him and into the stainless steel bowl was.

Red. So red.

It took him a while to stop the bleeding. He needed a couple of rags for that. He walked around Donnie again, then around Allie on his way to the bathroom. Wade and Rachel, their faces frozen in horror, watched him pass, the girl doing her best not to stare.

He turned on the bathroom lights and ignored Sabrina's body on the floor, where he had left her. Like her boyfriend, Sabrina had bled plenty afterward. He grabbed the first aid kit and opened it, then took a moment to look at his reflection in the mirror.

Well, he had certainly looked better, that was for sure.

That thought, for some reason, made him laugh out loud, even if every expelling of breath sent tremors across his face and added to the excruciating pain.

CHAPTER 11

THE TRICK TO dealing with pain wasn't to fight it. That only made things worse. Instead, the best approach was to accept it, to let it wash over you without resistance. Like a river, it was pointless to battle the current. It was easier to lie still and let the tide wash over you until, eventually, it dried up or, more likely, faded into the background.

Of course, learning what to do was different from actually putting that knowledge to use. As much as she tried to let the suffocating pain run its course without rising to defend against it, her instincts told her to battle back, to not let it have dominion over her. That only made things worse, and she grimaced with every jolt, every throbbing that seemed to pulse through her body like living electricity.

One of her ribs was broken. Or possibly two. But at least one; she knew that much because just breathing hurt. She could barely move before with the duct tape binding her wrists and ankles, and she had no chance of that now. Just thinking about moving an inch or two in any direction led her body to punish her further.

She was likely going to choke on her own blood pretty soon

anyway, which meant all of this had been for nothing. Wouldn't Carmen be disappointed when she learned how her big sister had screwed everything up and couldn't even avenge her death? Hell, big sister was going to die at the hands of the same man who had killed her.

The irony. Or was that tragedy?

Probably a little of both. Or a lot of both.

A shadow fell over her as Beckard returned and crouched. She managed to turn her head just far enough—which wasn't very far at all—to look up at him as he reached down and pulled the duct tape off her mouth with one merciless ripping motion.

She would have screamed if she had the strength. Instead, she just coughed up gobs of thick dark-red blood onto the floorboards.

"Wouldn't want you to choke on your own blood and die too quickly," Beckard said. His words were slightly slurred by the bloodied rag pressed against his broken nose. "You and I aren't going to say good-bye just yet, missy. That's one thing you'll be able to brag about after this: That I spent more time with you than I did with your little sister; hell, than all my other girls."

She coughed and spat out another thick stream of blood. Allie had to jerk her head back slightly to keep from lying in the collected pool. It didn't even look like something that had come out of her. It had the appearance of brown chocolate pudding left out in the sun. She almost gagged at the smell.

Beckard tore off a fresh piece of duct tape and slapped it over her mouth. Then he stood up and walked off.

"You, on the other hand," Beckard was saying.

Despite the rippling pain, Allie managed to roll over onto her other side so she could see Beckard crouching in front of

Wade and Rachel. Though he only had eyes for the girl.

Rachel was still trying in vain to disappear behind Wade, refusing to look or even acknowledge Beckard's presence. He didn't seem to mind or care. With the rag covering half his mouth, he looked like a shy woman hiding behind a veil. It would have been almost comical if it wasn't going to end so badly for all of them within the next few hours.

How much time did she have? The rest of the night, at least, and maybe part of the early morning. Beckard was indicating that he was going to take his time with her, but maybe that wasn't up to him. Sooner or later, someone was going to find their vehicles next to the highway. That would mean calls to the local authorities, maybe the same state troopers that Beckard claimed to be a part of.

She looked at his uniform again. The khaki shirt, the brown pants, and the silver star on his chest. Were those real? Was he really a state trooper? In all the research she had done on the man who had murdered her sister, she never once thought he could be a cop. He had hidden his identity that well. Her only comfort in having missed that very important detail was that the entire state police, along with the federal authorities that had swooped in to assist them, had also failed to uncover it.

Of course, that was small comfort now.

It made sense if she thought about it. It would explain how he had managed to elude the cops for so long. If he was one of them, he would know how they operated. But more importantly, he would have a front row seat on the investigation and would know if they were getting close to him and adapt.

He really is a cop, after all.

If he noticed her staring, he didn't acknowledge it. But then, he only had eyes for Rachel at the moment.

"Is it true what they say?" he was asking the girl. "Scars give a guy character?" He took away the rag to show off his broken nose and the layer of not-quite-drying blood around his mouth, like some grotesque clown's makeup. "I must have double the character after this, huh?"

Rachel didn't answer in any way. She had squeezed her eyes shut and seemed to be doing her best to pretend she couldn't see or hear Beckard.

See no evil, hear no evil, right, Rachel?

Beckard was chuckling. He was so satisfied with himself that he almost *(almost!)* didn't react in time when Wade lunged at him. Apparently Wade had taken a cue from Allie and was trying to deliver a second headbutt to Beckard's face. Allie could only imagine how effective it would have been had it landed. The young man might have even ended it right then and there.

Except Beckard had shut up and stumbled back just fast enough, his jerking motion more an exercise of self-preservation than anything remotely elegant. He sat down on his ass a few feet back while Wade flopped to the floor on his cheek in front of him with a loud *oomph*. The young man attempted to right himself, but it was difficult (Allie knew all about that) and he only managed to turn over onto his side.

Beckard picked himself up and brushed his hands on his pants. "Fool me once, shame on you. Fool me twice…well, you know how it goes." He glanced over and gave her an accusing look. "See what you did? I blame this on you. Kids always repeat what they see the adults do."

He walked back to the kitchen where he picked up another fresh rag. He soaked it under the sink faucet for a moment, wrung out most of the water, then dabbed it against his nose. He flinched once or twice, then picked up the shotgun and returned. She thought he might have been humming to himself the whole time. Some stupid pop song she had heard on the radio once or twice.

"I want to look good for her," he said, winking at Allie. "It's the least a man can do."

Rachel was staring, horrified, as Beckard walked back to her. Then she looked over at her boyfriend, still struggling to right himself. Not exactly the most heroic pose to a girl who had always depended on her boyfriend to hide behind, Allie guessed.

Beckard crouched next to Wade and pressed the barrel of the Remington against the young man's cheek. Wade went very still, as if afraid any sudden movement—or even breathing—might cause an accidental discharge. Rachel was crying, tears streaming down her face with the duct tape muffling any sounds she might have been making.

"I won't kill him," Beckard said to Rachel. "But I will, if you make me." He pulled back the shotgun and laid it across his knees. Wade's entire body sagged with relief. "But that doesn't mean I won't. It's up to you. Do you want me to put him out of his misery right now and get it over with?"

Rachel shook her head with urgency.

"Good; so we understand each other. Don't make me, and I won't. You won't make me, will you?"

Rachel seemed to consider the question. Maybe she didn't really understand it. Or maybe she did and wasn't sure about her answer.

"Well?" Beckard prompted. "Do we understand each other, missy?"

The girl finally nodded. That small movement seemed to take a lot out of her, and her body went slack afterward. Except for her eyes. They went to Wade, whose painfully constricted face said everything he couldn't.

Beckard looked satisfied and stood back up before holding out a hand toward Rachel.

Rachel looked as if she was about to vomit as she hesitantly lifted both bound arms toward him. He grabbed her by one wrist and, with a grin, pulled her up from the floor.

"That's a good girl," Beckard said. "Don't worry. I'll be nice. I'm always nice."

Until he's done with you. Then he's not so nice anymore.

I'm sorry, Rachel. I'm so sorry.

Rachel obviously didn't believe him either, because her entire body was trembling.

Beckard caressed one of her tear-streaked cheeks with two of his knuckles. He looked almost sympathetic, but she knew that was a lie. Sympathy was a human emotion, and there was nothing human about Beckard.

"Don't cry," Beckard cooed. "You're going to ruin those perfect cheekbones if you keep crying. We don't want that, do we? Let's be nice to each other—"

The sound of a barking dog shut him up.

Beckard spun around, suddenly forgetting that Rachel was there. Without Beckard to hold her up, the girl struggled in place for a moment before falling back down to the floor with a loud *thoomp!*

Outside the cabin, the barking was getting louder...because it was getting *closer*.

CHAPTER 12

HE SHOULD HAVE been pissed, but he wasn't. How could he be? The continued throbbing across the entire length and width of his face notwithstanding, things were still going better than he could have imagined given how the night had started out.

He should have been dead, but he wasn't.

Or arrested, but he wasn't.

A lot of things should have happened tonight, most of it not in his favor.

All things considered, it was still a pretty darn good night.

No, Beckard wasn't angry. He was a bit annoyed, though, but that quickly turned to curiosity as he stalked across the room and slid against the wall next to the window and peered out at the two figures approaching the front yard. A dog, mostly white with patches of brown fur, walked in front of them, barking up a storm. The animal looked like a shorter, skinnier version of a cow, one with long floppy ears. Its nose was pointed straight at the same window that Beckard was peering out of at the moment.

Both men wore camouflage hunting clothes, which made him wonder what they were doing out here at this time of the night. They both carried bolt-action rifles, and one was holding the dog by a leash and keeping the animal from bolting forward. Beckard guessed the little bastard could either smell him or had seen him peeking.

He glanced over at Allie. She was staring back at him, as if wondering what he was going to do next—and probably hoping it would lead to his death, no doubt. Rachel was still lying on the floor on her side, looking equally expectant. Wade had somehow managed to roll over to Rachel.

He turned back to the window.

The dog was still barking, though all three figures had stopped in the middle of the yard next to the minivan. The hunter with the cap was trying to look through the vehicle's tinted windows, the same way Beckard had earlier.

"Hello in there!" the man with the dog called out. He was a few inches shorter than his buddy but looked a few grizzled years older. They were both wearing dirt-caked boots to complete their hunting ensemble. "We found your vehicles near the highway!" the man continued. "Wanted to see if anyone was hurt and needed assistance!"

A good Samaritan. Just my luck.

Beckard leaned away from the window and didn't answer.

He looked over at Donnie's corpse in the kitchen, half-visible behind the counter. Over to his right were Allie and the lovebirds, bound and gagged. Yup. There was no way he could let the hunters into the cabin. Maybe if he flashed his badge…and then what? They had come from the highway. They had seen the vehicles. And chances were they had tracked him by his blood, the same way Allie had.

So what did they know? Probably not much.

What did they suspect? Probably a lot.

The big question was: Why hadn't they called the police yet?

"Hello?" the man called out again. "We can see the lights. We know someone's inside."

Beckard moved alongside the wall toward the front door. There was a peephole, and he used it now.

The older hunter was still in the front yard with his dog. The animal had ceased its barking and now sat obediently on its haunches, waiting for orders. Beckard couldn't locate the second man, and that immediately set off alarms in his head.

Where'd you go, buddy?

Beckard changed his angle and spotted the minivan's hood to the right of the hunter and his dog. He still couldn't locate the second man. Where did the guy go? Was he trying to circle around the cabin? Maybe looking for a back way in? *Was* there a back way in? It wasn't as if Beckard had checked. It had never seemed especially important because he had already achieved total control of the building.

Shit. There better not be a back door.

"Hello!" the hunter shouted again. It sounded as if he was starting to lose his patience.

Tough nuts, buddy.

"Look, I know someone's in there," the man continued. "I saw you moving next to the window."

Beckard peered through the peephole again, looking left, then right, as far as the small opening would allow him. There was still just the wide-open yard and the man standing in the middle of it with his dog.

Where did the second guy go?

"I'm just looking to help!" the man shouted. "We have a

phone. If you need it, we can call the cops for you." He paused, then, "We're not leaving until someone comes outside and talks to us."

The problem was the door. It wasn't locked. There was a chain lock, but it had broken when Allie busted inside like John Wayne earlier. If the guy really wanted to come in, he was going to come in.

Where the hell is the second guy?

Beckard ducked and went on his hands and knees and crawled back across the room, staying under the windowsill. He glanced over and saw Allie looking after him, and he couldn't be sure, but she looked almost...amused?

He finished crawling to the other side of the window. He stood up—too fast—and winced at the pain from his side. He had to put one hand against the wall to support himself until the sensation passed. It took its time, too. With the broken nose and the pain spread liberally across his face, he had forgotten all about his side. For a while there, anyway.

"I'm calling the cops!" the man shouted from outside. "If no one's coming out to talk to me, I'm going to let them sort this mess out."

The man hadn't finished saying the word "out" when Beckard heard the very clear sounds of boots moving on the floorboards behind him. He turned around and lifted the shotgun just as the tall, lanky hunter with the cap appeared out of the back hallway, his eyes shifting automatically to the three bound people on the floor in front of him. The sight was clearly something he hadn't expected, and the man stared for exactly two seconds.

It was one second more than Beckard needed.

Beckard fired, and buckshot ripped apart chunks of the hallway along with the man's head.

He turned around—again, too fast, and cursed under his breath at the stabbing pain—and sidestepped until he was standing in front of the window. He looked out, saw the other hunter trying to unsling his rifle, reacting to the sound of gunshot, while his dog began barking again.

The man saw Beckard at about the same time and he dived sideways as Beckard fired, shattering the window into a thousand pieces and sending glass shards everywhere. Buckshot *pinged!* against the hood of the minivan as the figure slipped behind it.

Beckard was racking the shotgun when he saw the dog—all white with patches of brown fur and sharp, salivating white teeth—racing across the yard. Then the animal did something Beckard didn't anticipate and launched itself—

What the hell?

He was still trying to process the sight of the animal leaping through the air like some kind of furry missile when it entered through the shattered window and barreled into his chest headfirst.

Beckard went flying backward, cursing in his head even if he couldn't get the sounds out. He was still awed by the fact that the dog had managed to run across the open ground and jumped into the cabin before he could fire a third shot. All that took a backseat when bursting pain rippled across his body from his broken nose to his chest, where the animal had slammed into him, and all the way down to his side, which may or may not have started bleeding again behind the gauze wrapping.

What the fuck *is happening?*

And the shotgun was gone. It had flown out of his hands at

the same time the dog smashed into him like a baseball bat and sent him flopping to the floor on his back. Then his entire world shrank, with nothing but the slobbering beast on top of him trying to bite his face off occupying his frayed senses.

Beckard somehow managed to get his left arm under the dog's chin. He pushed with everything he had—and digging deep down for more—just to keep the animal at bay. Its teeth (*Jesus Christ, they're sharp!*) were snapping, trying to get at him even as he struggled against its surging, furry body.

Beckard managed to draw his knife with his free hand. He jerked his arm back and was about to drive it through the mutt's head when a loud whistle cut through the air. The animal pulled back, cocking its head slightly to one side, just before it leaped off Beckard. The dog spun around and, showing amazing fluidity, jumped through the window and disappeared outside.

He stared at the window, sucking in one labored breath after another, the knife in his fist still poised to strike in case the creature came back in through the same opening for a second go at his face.

But it didn't, and Beckard gathered himself and scrambled up from the floor. Or stumbled and fell and hobbled, anyway. However he did it, he wasn't helplessly lying on his back anymore, and though his entire body was on fire from head to toe (he couldn't blink without something hurting), at least he still *had* a face.

He had managed to make it onto his hands and knees when he glanced around the cabin and saw the shotgun a few yards away. Wade and Rachel were staring longingly at it, and Wade might have even managed to roll toward it just a little bit because he wasn't where Beckard last remembered him. Or maybe he was just imagining things. It was hard to concentrate through the misery that was swarming all of his senses at the moment.

He crawled toward the shotgun and picked it up, then hurried back to the wall and leaned next to the window. If the dog charged again, Beckard would have a clear shot at the animal before it located him. Then he'd see how the little bastard liked a face full of buckshot.

Suck on some lead, Fido!

He wanted to laugh, but he didn't. He couldn't. It hurt too much just to think about laughing, much less actually going through with it.

Beckard wiped at sweat and what he thought might have been dog saliva on his face and forehead. Ugh. The lingering smell made him want to gag, but he had enough control left of his body to fight against that urge.

"Marcus!" The other hunter shouted from outside. "You in there? Marcus!"

He looked over at the hallway, where there was apparently another way into the cabin somewhere back there because the tall hunter *(Marcus, I presume)* had found it. The only part of Marcus that he could see were his legs and mud-caked boots sticking out of the narrow passageway. No signs of his rifle, but it was probably in there somewhere. Beckard's buckshot had torn big chunks out of the wall but had also gotten enough of the man to finish him off.

From outside: "Goddammit, Marcus, answer me!"

He's dead, asshole. Buy a clue.

He glanced across the room at Allie. She was watching him back, still trying to stab him to death with her eyes. He smiled despite himself. He admired her grit and determination. If it wasn't for Rachel, he would have devoted all the time he had left to her. He had a feeling she would be worth it.

And sisters, too. That was a new one. But maybe, if it worked out, he might try it again, except this time on purpose—

His head snapped back to the window when he heard the sound. He knew immediately what it was even before the beast flashed by next to his head. Fur and spittle and the smell of an animal who spent too much time in the muck and stink of the outdoors overwhelmed him in a split instant.

The dog landed in front of him and whirled around as if it were chasing its own tail. The animal looked confused as it tried to reacquire him.

Ha! Stupid dog!

He was about to shoot the mutt when the door opened with a *crash!* and the hunter stumbled inside. The man must have been moving too fast, likely charged up with adrenaline, because he seemed to lose his balance. The sight of him staggering through the open doorway was almost comical.

Of course, Beckard didn't get the chance to LOL (or even LMFBO) at that moment, either.

He fired, and so did the hunter.

At the same time, the dog was growling right next to him, clearly indicating that the beast had, finally, found him again.

Oh, hell.

CHAPTER 13

IT WAS A piece of glass. Beckard didn't see it, and there was no reason he should have. It was so small she would have missed it if she hadn't been lying on her stomach staring at it, sticking out from between one of the floorboards just a foot from her head. If she had to guess (not that she spent all that long thinking about it), it had broken off when Beckard shot Donnie in the kitchen. She remembered seeing a glass on the counter, and then it wasn't there anymore.

She reached up with her bound hands, ignoring the stinging pain rippling up and down from her waist to her neck, and palmed the piece of glass. It was barely an inch long and half an inch wide, so it fit perfectly into her palm when she pulled her hands back into position in front of her.

It was impossible to use the glass to cut her hands free. Even if she could somehow angle it into position—*upward* toward her wrists—she simply didn't have the leverage for the seesaw motion required. So instead, she let her hands fall toward her bound feet. She spun the shard so the sharper edge was facing the duct tape.

Then she began cutting.

Slowly. Oh so slowly so she wouldn't make a sound, because glass sliding against duct tape did make a sound. Too loud, though a part of her knew that was only because she was listening for it. Chances were it wasn't *that* loud, but she couldn't risk it.

Not now. Not now...

Thank God the man with the dog showed up. Or men. Because she heard the voice outside keep referring to "we," which meant there was more than one out there. How many? And what exactly were they doing walking around the woods with a dog at almost midnight?

Or was it midnight already? Early morning? It didn't feel that way. Then again, pain had a way of dulling your senses, making you lose track of time. It was a little hard to care about what was happening outside when your insides were on fire.

And right now, it felt as if her body was trying to burn its way inside out, because Beckard had been vicious. She didn't think he would ever stop kicking her. She was certain he was going to kill her, and the only reason he didn't, she guessed, was because he had tired himself out.

She had a second chance now. The men outside had given her that opportunity to turn this around, to *survive*. Their presence drew all of Beckard's attention and he was barely looking at her, or Wade and Rachel. Even when he did, his attention was quickly pulled away again.

When he turned his back to her in order to look out the door's peephole, she really got to work slicing away at the duct tape. She kept her hands in front of her at all times even when she wasn't cutting so Beckard would get used to the sight. It seemed to work, because each time he looked over he remained clueless.

Almost there…

Beckard gave up on the door and returned to the window. She stopped cutting, waited for him to turn his back to her again, and when he did, resumed the back and forth. Just small motions, nothing that would be too obvious.

Careful. Careful…

She was halfway through when she heard footsteps and turned her head and saw a tall man in some kind of camo clothing and a cap stepping out of the back hallway. He was holding a rifle and made the mistake of staring at Wade and Rachel for just a second too long.

Boom!

The man's head disintegrated, along with pieces of the hallway around him, as Beckard fired the shotgun. The sight of a man's head disappearing—carved away by buckshot—was a surreal experience, even more so than when Beckard had murdered Donnie in front of her. It startled her for a brief second, and she might have even gasped out loud. Or as out loud as she could muster against the duct tape over her mouth.

Then Beckard fired again, this time at the window.

Glass shattered, and there was a loud growling sound and when she looked up, Allie couldn't believe her eyes as a dog flew through the rectangular opening where the window used to be and smashed into Beckard. Man and beast fell to the floor in a pile and—

The shotgun!

It flew out of Beckard's hands as he landed on his back, the shock of the animal attack apparently more traumatic for him to experience than it had been for her to witness.

Allie willed herself to look away from Beckard and the dog and instead concentrated on the duct tape. She began slicing faster and faster and faster still—

A loud whistle pierced the air, coming from outside.

She looked up just in time to see the dog leaping back through the window and disappearing into the dark night.

No, no, no! You stupid dog, where are you going? Get back here!

Just when she had almost convinced herself all was not lost, that she didn't need the dog to save the day, she saw Beckard crawling back to the wall *with the shotgun in his hands*. He leaned next to the broken window and sucked in large gulps of air. Almost as an afterthought, he looked across the cabin at her.

Allie quickly folded the piece of glass back into her palm and glared back at him.

Beckard smirked, then looked to his left, back at the window just as *the dog leapt back inside!*

God, that is one amazing dog, Allie thought just as the door in front of her opened with a *crash!* and a man, also wearing camo clothing like the one who was missing his head, stumbled inside. The man must have lost his balance as he came through the door, because he careened slightly forward while at the same time gripping a bolt-action rifle in his hands. She wondered if she looked that silly when she had barged inside earlier.

The hunter spun to his right and fired from the hip at almost the same time Allie heard the Remington roar from the other side of the cabin. The stocky man in the mud-caked boots took almost all of the buckshot in the chest and was flung into the door. The rifle fell from his hands as he slid down, lifeless, but by then Allie was already turning at the sound of—

The dog had its mouth clamped over Beckard's right arm,

between the wrist and the elbow. Beckard was desperately trying to hold onto the shotgun even as he was spinning his body wildly from left to right and back again, trying to dislodge the animal. It wasn't going to work. The dog, like a small furry child, was trying to pull Beckard to the floor and down to its level. If it managed that, then it would be over.

Come on, dog! He just killed your master! Pull him down and sink your teeth into his neck! Come on, dammit!

Allie looked back at the hunter. Dead. More than dead. *Really* dead. She tried not to focus on the holes in his chest where the buckshot had torn into him or the thick, fresh pool of blood gathering under him. Instead, she located the rifle that had fallen to the floor before abandoning it completely when she glimpsed the pistol in the man's hip holster.

She went back to frantically cutting the duct tape, this time putting everything she had into it without worrying about being caught. She was almost there. She was so close! A little more. Just a little mo—

Snap! She jerked both legs in opposite directions, then dropped the glass shard and scrambled up, wasting a precious half second to pull the duct tape off her mouth. She sucked in a big breath and didn't realize what a luxury just being able to breathe was.

The gun! Go for the gun!

She ran and was halfway to the dead hunter when she sneaked a look back at Beckard. He had dropped the shotgun and was desperately trying to keep the animal back with his bare hands. Blood dripped like a faucet down his arms, streams of it flooding the dog's mouth and chin and splashing white and brown fur on its way to the floor. It was a ghastly sight, but it also made Allie's heart sing.

Kill him, dog! Bite his hand off! Bite the whole thing off!

If Beckard was even aware of her, he didn't show it. He was too busy with other things at the moment, like trying to keep the dog from chewing his arm off at the bone. The animal's growls filled the cabin, and Allie was only vaguely aware of Wade and Rachel struggling against their bindings on the floor, the young man trying to get up but falling back down in almost comical fashion.

Allie blocked everything out and focused on the gun.

There!

She practically dived the last few feet, sliding to the floor on her knees in front of the dead man, who sat against the door like he had simply taken a nap. She grabbed the handgun with both hands—not like she had a choice, since her wrists were still bound—and jerked it free from the holster. It came out smoothly, the smell of well-oiled metal against leather filling her nostrils. She inhaled it, thankful to be able to smell anything at all after coughing up so much blood earlier.

Still on her knees, she turned, the finger of one hand fumbling with the side of the weapon for the safety switch. She wasted a precious second staring at Beckard as he staggered toward the window, having somehow dislodged himself from the dog when she wasn't looking. He was cradling his mauled right arm with his left and looked like a drunk stumbling home after a long night of drinking. Thick patches of blood splattered the floor, leaving a bloody red trail as he backpedaled. The shotgun was on the floor, beyond his reach, and she wondered if he even remembered it through the obvious pain.

Wait. The dog. Where was the dog?

It was on the floor, all the way across the cabin where Beckard had tossed it after somehow having managed to dislodge it. The dog was attempting to right itself, scrambling furiously to find its footing, and would no doubt be hurling itself right back at Beckard to finish the job at any second.

Not if I finish him off first, dog!

Beckard turned and their eyes locked.

For a moment, just a brief moment, she thought he might grin or wink at her, but there was just pain—overwhelming and miserable pain—on his face. His eyes shifted from hers and to the gun in her hand.

She lifted the gun and took aim, squeezing the trigger.

The first bullet must have missed him by only a few inches because Beckard snapped his head around as if he had been shot. She blamed it on her bound hands throwing off her aim.

She started to squeeze the trigger again when Beckard spun around, as if he were doing some kind of absurd pirouette, and dived through the window. Her second shot hit the wall where he had been standing just half a second ago.

No!

Allie stumbled to her feet and ran across the room. She had forgotten about the pain in her gut and the broken ribs. Right now, the only thing that mattered was getting to the window and catching Beckard before he could escape.

She aimed the gun out the window and swept from left to right, looking into the yard, with only the minivan to break the monotony of darkness.

But there was no Beckard.

Through the hard breathing and the dizzying adrenaline surging through her, she managed to spot the thick red drops of blood covering the windowsill, running in a jagged line along the ground outside. The red and black trail curved around the minivan and kept going.

No!

She didn't dare lower the gun yet, even though she knew without actually knowing that he was gone.

She'd had him, and she had lost him. *Again.*

She wasn't sure how long it took—maybe a few seconds, or a few minutes—for her to finally gather herself. Slowly, her breathing stopped coming out in spurts and she became aware of everything around her again.

Allie turned around and almost stepped on the dog. It was jogging briskly toward its master—her, Beckard, and everything else apparently forgotten. She watched it attempt to nudge the hunter awake with its nose, and when that didn't work, the animal lay down on its stomach and licked the dead man's hand before it let out what sounded like a soft, sorrowful cry.

Even a dog, she thought, possessed more humanity than Beckard ever would.

CHAPTER 14

THIS WAS IT.

The straw that broke the camel's back.

The end of the road.

The light at the end of the tunnel.

The...

Jesus, he couldn't even come up with four clichés? If he didn't know he was in deep shit before, then this pretty much confirmed it. Not being able to come up with four clichés about how up a creek without a paddle he was—

Number four!

He laughed. LOL? Maybe. Or perhaps just a light chuckle at the least. Then again, he might have just opened his mouth and wheezed out some labored breath that had nothing to do with laughing or anything beyond breathing. It was hard to tell at the moment.

He wasn't even convinced he was actually still alive. All of this could have been a figment of his imagination, something his fevered mind had conjured up just to occupy him as he lay in the front yard of the cabin, dying from his wounds.

Buckshot in the side.

Broken nose.

Right hand…

Did he even have a right hand anymore?

He peeked at it now, not sure he wanted to actually see what was down there, if anything. His hand *seemed* to still be attached under the khaki shirt he was using as a tourniquet. It looked more like a giant loaf of bread, albeit one that was *drip-drip-dripping* blood as he trudged through the woods without any real direction. Or a shirt on, for that matter. For some reason, though, he barely felt the cold. He blamed *(thanked)* his body's general numbness for that.

Apparently this was his life now—staggering through un-known woods while trying not to bleed to death.

What a life.

At least it was still night out, if the suffocating darkness around him was any indication. And he was far, far from the nearest highway, so all those gunshots probably went unnoticed. It was why he had chosen this area—or, well, the general vicinity, anyway—to do his work in the first place. It was even more desolate two miles down the road where everything would have worked out fine if he had taken her as planned. Of course, he'd had no idea she had come prepared.

Goddamn, she had come prepared!

And yet, things were working out anyway despite all his bungling. He had convinced those college kids *(Kids these days are dumber than bags of rocks, amirite?)*, somehow managed to get the upper hand on Allie *(Who's in charge now, bitch?)*, and was about to have a little fun with not one, but two people who perfectly fit his ideal type when…

The two hunters.

What was that one of them had said back at the cabin?

"We found your vehicles near the highway! Wanted to see if anyone was hurt and needed assistance!"

The truck.

My truck.

He stopped for a moment and looked around him. Really, really looked around him instead of just stumbling along like a blind fool. He focused on his surroundings for the first time since he had crashed into the woods back at the cabin.

Every tree looked like the other hundred trees he had walked past, and every stretch of ground looked identical to—

I'm lost. I'm so lost.

Christ on a stick.

If he could only find his truck again. His, or the hunters'. Or maybe even Allie's car. It didn't matter as long as it worked. All he had to do was get to one of them. That, unfortunately, was easier said than done. Especially out here, at night, with no signs of—

There!

It was the sound of a car moving somewhere in the distance. It came out of the blue, like a sliver of hope, and then it was gone again. But it had been there just long enough—maybe half a second—for him to turn in its direction.

The highway. It was a car driving down the highway.

He began moving toward the origin of the sound. Or where he thought it had come from.

Let me be right. Come on, God, just this once. Have I ever asked you for anything? Besides letting me kill those girls, I mean?

He might have laughed then.

Or cackled.

Or maybe just let out another haggard wheeze.

THE TRUCK.

All he had to do was reach it before he bled to death in this godforsaken stretch of abandoned woods. Well, not abandoned, exactly. There was that cabin, and those two hunters clearly knew the area, so maybe they lived around here. Maybe he could find their house or cabin or hideout and rest for a while. Wouldn't that be ideal?

Now *that* was worthy of an LOL.

And he would have laughed out loud too, if not for the fresh jolt of pain that made his entire body quiver for a few seconds. Who knew getting shot, then having your nose smashed in, and then getting mauled by a dog could hurt so much?

He did, now.

He pushed on anyway, because there was no other choice.

Keep moving, chum. That's right, keep moving.

One foot at a time.

One foot at a time…

Whenever he thought he might have gone in the wrong direction, he heard what sounded like vehicles moving in front of him. Not right in front of him, of course—that would have been way too easy—but further away.

Cars.

Or, at least, he thought he was hearing cars. Which didn't really make a lot of sense. This was a lonely stretch of road that cut through the middle of nowhere. The last piece of civilization was almost twenty miles back up the road, and there wasn't anything on the other side until twenty-five miles later. That was why he had chosen this area, after all.

Not completely true. The cabin, remember?

Right. The cabin. He hadn't known it was there until tonight. This wasn't prime hunting ground, so most people stayed away, which meant those hunters had to have stumbled across the vehicles while they were driving on the highway, but for some reason decided to stop and investigate.

Good Samaritans with rifles. And a dog. Just what he needed.

Pfft.

They had ruined things, not just with the college kids, but with Allie, too.

He still remembered the taste of her sister, Carmen. Everything about her had been perfect. The blonde hair, the blue eyes, and the slender figure. Carmen had been twenty or twenty-one (*Which one was it? Can't remember*) when he took her…how long ago now? Too long ago, back when he was still young and new at this. He had been sloppy back then. Was that how the sister tracked him down? Using those early days, finding mistakes he didn't know he had made?

She was smart, that one.

And feisty. Just my type.

Too bad he'd have to kill her. He would have liked nothing better than to keep her around a little longer, but that wasn't going to happen. At least, not if he wanted to get out of this with his head still attached to his shoulders.

Now that she'd failed to kill him, he had no doubts she would settle for exposing him. He would have to go on the run.

Start all over again somewhere. Maybe Mexico. He was fond of Mexican beer. It tasted like piss, sure, but you could fix that with a little Tabasco sauce…

HE FOUND IT.

The truck.

It was parked in the woods with the highway in the background exactly where he had left it. The white Ford was also there, with its shattered driver-side window. In the moonlight, he fancied he could actually see his own blood spatter along the hood of the vehicle where he had done his *Dukes of Hazzard* slide to keep from being perforated by her shotgun blast.

He expected to see all those things, but not the two state troopers.

One uniformed figure was shining a flashlight into the front seat of his truck through the window, while the second one was inside the Ford going through the glove compartment.

He thought about turning and fleeing back into the woods, but then what? He was weak, half-dead, and he wouldn't have gotten far. At least this way he could beat Allie to the punch. He had been pretty damn convincing with the kids, and he didn't even know them. These guys, on the other hand, they were his brothers.

Hey, it worked once before…

Beckard stumbled out of the woods, *crunching* grass under his shoes and making as much noise as possible. The last thing he needed was to get shot again.

The trooper peering into the truck saw him first and shined

his flashlight into Beckard's face while at the same time drawing his sidearm. "Hold it right there, mister!"

Beckard stopped and threw up both hands, even though doing so caused a tremendous tidal wave of pain to wash over him. He gritted his teeth through it and shouted back, "Don't shoot! Don't shoot!"

The other trooper back-crawled out of the Ford and rounded the hood, his hand resting on the butt of his sidearm. He also shined his flashlight in Beckard's face before lowering it to Beckard's right arm, then finally down to his exposed gauze-wrapped side.

"Stay right there until I reach you," the first trooper said. He stepped closer before a spark of recognition spread across his face. "Holy shit. Is that you, Beckard? Where's your shirt?"

Beckard lowered his arms and sighed with relief. "Yeah, it's me, Pratt. Can you guys get me to a hospital? I think I'm about to bleed to death here."

He sat down on the ground and leaned back against a tree. Gnarled bark pricked at his bare back, but it was nothing compared to the pain coming from the rest of his body, so he easily ignored it.

He was tired. So, so tired.

Pratt and the other state trooper, whom Beckard recognized as Barnes, moved toward him. Barnes was talking into his radio while Pratt crouched next to him and shined his flashlight in Beckard's face again before lowering the beam to his bare chest, then to the shirt wrapped around his bloody arm.

"Jesus Christ, what the hell happened to you?" Pratt asked.

Yeah, I can definitely make this work…

"There was a woman," Beckard said. "She's dangerous, and she has a shotgun…"

CHAPTER 15

THE GIRL WAS shaking as Allie removed the duct tape from her mouth, then used the knife she had gotten from the kitchen to cut her free.

"Stay here," she told Rachel. "The both of you."

Rachel nodded and scooted over to Wade as Allie did the same to his binds.

He sucked in a large grateful breath, then asked, "Where are you going?"

"After him," Allie said.

"You're crazy. That guy's a maniac."

"That's why I'm going after him."

Rachel was glued to the dog across the room, still sitting next to its owner. If it was aware of their existence inside the cabin, it didn't show it. She wondered if it knew its master was dead. Or did it think he was just sleeping? How smart was a dog, anyway?

"Should we..." Rachel started to say.

"Leave it alone," Allie said.

"You saw the way it clamped down on his arm?" Wade said. "I can't believe he's still walking around out there after that."

Allie turned to the window and peered out at the darkness

again. Wade was right. Beckard was out there, somewhere. The way he had been bleeding all night, it was a miracle the man was even still alive. If she was lucky, he had fallen unconscious somewhere in the woods not far from here and all she'd have to do was track him down and put him out of his misery.

If I'm lucky. Because I've been really lucky tonight.

Yeah, right.

She looked back at the college students. "Rachel, do you still have your phone?"

The girl nodded and pulled her cell phone out of her pocket and handed it over. "Do you really think he called the police earlier?"

"I don't know, but we can find out."

Allie took the phone and punched up the calls list. The most recent was less than two hours ago. It wasn't, as she had expected, 911, but a string of numbers that looked almost random. She pressed redial and put the call on speaker.

A computerized voice answered. "The number you have dialed is no longer in service. Please hang up and try again."

She ended the call. "I guess not."

"Was he even really a cop?" Wade asked.

Good question.

She had been trying to figure that one out since Beckard revealed himself in his state trooper's uniform. If he really was law enforcement, it explained so many things, but she couldn't pretend as if he wasn't capable of another lie. Beckard had proven all night just what a good liar he was.

"I don't know," Allie said. "I spent so many years looking for him, studying everything he's done that the cops and the papers knew about. Not once did it occur to me that he might have been a cop. A state trooper. But it makes sense, now that I think about it."

"You've been searching for him," Wade said. It wasn't a question. "How long?"

"Ten years." She pulled the handgun out of her waistband and walked to the window, letting the chilly air wash over her. "How far are we from the highway, Wade?"

"A mile, maybe," Wade said. Then, "Aren't you going to call the cops?"

Allie looked down at the phone.

"Ma'am?" Wade said.

She was surprised by that, but then realized he wasn't wrong. She was thirty-three and at least ten years older than him. Wade looked barely twenty-one, maybe twenty-two at the most. He was just a kid.

Like Donnie, dead in the kitchen.

Or Sabrina, in the bathroom.

Like Carmen...

Beckard's victims. That was the point of tonight—to keep him from taking more lives. But she had screwed that up, and Donnie and Sabrina had taken the brunt of that failure. And he was still out there, right now...

You can run but you can't hide, you sonofabitch.

"Not yet," Allie said. She walked back over and tossed the phone to Wade. "Give me until dawn."

"Dawn?" Wade said, confused.

"Before you call the cops."

Wade exchanged a worried glance with Rachel. Then he looked back at her. "Why? What are you going to do between now and dawn?"

"I'm going to hunt him down."

"But why? He's gone. All we have to do is call the cops and wait for them to show up. The *real* cops. They'll take care of it. Take care of him."

"It's safer that way," Rachel said, clutching Wade's arm.

Allie handed the pistol to Wade, who took it hesitantly.

"He killed my sister," Allie said. "And he just killed your friends."

Wade's eyes darted to Donnie's half-visible body in the kitchen.

"Do you know what the cops will do when they find him?" Allie asked. "They're going to put him in prison and he's going to sit there and wait for a year—if we're lucky—while he goes on trial. More likely, he'll spend years inside with a nice comfortable bed, eating three meals a day and exercising in the yard, while the trial drags on and he becomes a celebrity. Girls will send him letters, and he'll smile for the camera and mock everything that's decent. Even if he's convicted, there will be appeals. A lot of them. Five years, maybe more, until he gets what he deserves for killing your friends. For killing my sister. For killing all the other sisters and wives and nieces."

She paused for a few seconds to let her words sink in.

"Do you want that?" she continued. "Can the two of you live with that? I can't. It took me a long time to get here. Trust me when I tell you, you don't want to live the next five or ten years waiting for him to get what he's got coming. That's no way to live."

Wade's face had slowly hardened as she talked, and she knew she had gotten through to him. He looked over at Rachel and, to Allie's surprise, the younger woman nodded, her own face looking just as grim and determined.

She's a lot tougher than I gave her credit for.

"Okay," Wade said. "We won't call the police until dawn. That should give you enough time to hunt the sonofabitch down."

Allie nodded gratefully, then walked over and picked the shotgun up from the floor. Wade and Rachel watched her curiously as she reloaded the weapon with the extra shells from the side carrier.

"I won't be coming back to the cabin, Wade," Allie said. "If you hear someone coming and there aren't police sirens, you should shoot first and ask questions later."

Wade stood up from the floor, pulling Rachel with him. "We'll be fine," the young man said. "Don't let the bastard get away."

She smiled at them and walked to the open door.

Allie stopped next to the dog. It lifted its head slightly and looked up at her with large brown eyes. Was it asking her a question? Maybe about its master?

She crouched next to the animal and stroked its head, forgetting that less than ten minutes ago it had tried to bite its way through Beckard's arm. It might have sighed (did dogs sigh?), before laying its head down on its chin to let her run her fingers through thick, blood-matted fur. Beckard's blood.

I hope you're bleeding to death out there right now, you piece of shit.

She put her palm in front of the dog's head and the animal licked it. "Stay, boy. Stay with your master."

It seemed to groan in response, then returned its stare to its unmoving owner.

She stood up and left the cabin.

Her side still hurt, and the ribs that Beckard had broken made her wince with every step. She hadn't felt the pain when she was running around earlier, thanks to the abundant adrenaline. It was gone now, and she couldn't avoid it any longer. And she didn't want to. Pain helped her concentrate on the moment, on what awaited her out there.

I'm coming for you, Beckard.

Every step, every breath, reminded her of those ten years of research, the six years of training, and the three years getting ready for this one moment. She thought it had passed after the bad turn earlier, but things had reset. She had a second (third?) chance, and the night wasn't over yet.

It didn't take her very long to pick up his trail. All she had to do was follow the bloody drops, still fresh, on the grass. They led her around the minivan, where she spotted handprints along the side of the vehicle. How the man was even still alive, much less fleeing while bleeding like this, was mindboggling. Maybe, like her, he was just determined not to die until the job was done.

She found the spot where he had returned into the woods and followed.

THE FLASHLIGHT BEAM came out of nowhere and hit her in the face as soon as she stepped out of the trees and into the clearing, where she had tracked Beckard's blood trail.

He was going back to the side of the highway, returning to the spot where their vehicles had crashed last night. She had no idea how he even knew what directions to take, but maybe the man was just better at moving around in the woods than she gave him credit for.

None of that mattered now as the brightness blinded her and she instinctively lifted the shotgun to fire.

Allie was on the verge of pulling the trigger when she heard a man's voice *(not Beckard)* screaming through a bullhorn, "State police! Lower your weapon, or we will open fire!"

It's not Beckard's voice! her mind shouted.

Don't shoot!

You're going to kill cops!

In the back of her mind, another voice screamed, *What if they're like Beckard? Don't take the chance!*

Through the blind spots she saw not one, or two, but what seemed like half a dozen figures standing in a semicircle, their flashlights and the headlights of multiple vehicles pointed right at her as if they knew exactly where she would emerge out of the woods and had been lying in wait all this time.

But of course they knew. She was following the blood trail that Beckard had left behind.

Beckard!

She couldn't tell if the figures had their weapons drawn, but it was a damn good chance they did.

"Lower your weapon now!" the voice boomed again. "You're surrounded! Lower your weapon, or we will open fire on you!"

No, no, I was so close.

I was so close!

Allie lowered her arms slowly, expecting the first gunshot to ring out and the first bullet to strike her. She had seen stories like this on TV. All it took was one trigger-happy cop and it was over. The irony was that she wouldn't have blamed them. She had just burst out of the woods with a shotgun, after all. Shooting her down now would have been completely justified.

She kept waiting for the bullet, for the loud crash of a gunshot, but they didn't come.

Instead, the lights continued to blind her mercilessly even as Allie bent her knees slowly and placed the shotgun on the ground. As soon as she did that, three of the shadowy figures rushed forward. They swarmed her, one almost tackling her as he pushed her down with his much bigger body. She grunted through the pain, wondered if maybe she had just broken another rib.

A pair of large hands ripped the shotgun from her grip while their owners shouted, "I got it! I got the weapon!"

You got it because I let you have it, asshole! she wanted to shout back, but of course she couldn't because there was suddenly a knee pressing down on the small of her back and her face was buried in grass and dirt.

Callous hands seized her arms, followed by the cold sting of metal handcuffs snapping into place and biting into her wrists. She grimaced through the assault, but it was nothing compared to the burning fire roaring up and down her sides.

Finally, the one on top backed off and she could breathe again.

"This her?" she heard a voice she didn't recognize ask.

"Yeah, that's her," another voice answered. This one sounded familiar.

She turned her head sideways. Two of the state troopers were standing behind her, their legs blocking her view of another man in the background. She didn't have to see his face to know who it was.

She recognized his voice easily enough.

"That looks like the shotgun she tried to kill me with," Beckard said.

Then, when the two troopers bent to haul her from the ground like she was a piece of useless meat, Beckard took the moment to wink at her.

CHAPTER 16

TROOPER JONES WASN'T going to be a problem, but Sergeant Harper, the shift supervisor, was another story. Beckard knew both men well enough to be indifferent of Jones and very, very wary of Harper.

"Tell me again," Harper was saying from the front passenger seat of the Crown Victoria. "What were you doing out there in the middle of the night with a knife?"

Beckard sat in the back of the vehicle, on the wrong side of a fourteen-gauge steel partition. The setup had been good enough to haul around criminals for the last ten years or so, and it was still good now. Not that Beckard had any ideas about escaping.

Not yet, anyway. They were on their way to the closest hospital nearly twenty-five miles away, which he was very thankful for. Once he got his wounds taken care of and was satisfied he wasn't going to die tonight, he could then decide how to proceed. Besides, he was too busy grimacing through the pain, which ironically probably made his story more convincing to Harper, who kept a close eye on him by way of the rearview mirror.

Or, at least, Beckard hoped he was being convincing. Harper

was a hard-ass, so there was always a chance he wasn't buying it. It was difficult to tell from the man's facial expression, which looked permanently frozen in a state of being pissed off.

"I had the knife in my truck, Sarge," Beckard said. "It's a good thing, too. I was coming home from Rita's when she came out of nowhere and almost sideswiped me. I figured she was drunk and chased her, tried to flag her down before she did the same thing to some poor sap on the highway, but she wouldn't stop. I ended up having to PIT her, and we went flying into the woods."

"Why didn't you call for backup?" Harper asked.

"No time. I did what I thought I had to at the time."

"And the shotgun?"

"She had it in her car. Don't ask me what she was doing with it. Maybe you can get her to talk later at the station."

"I'll do that."

Did the sergeant looked convinced? Maybe semi-convinced?

Damn, it was hard to read the guy.

"Cold back there?" Jones asked with a grin.

Beckard snorted. Although he hadn't felt the cold while he was stumbling his way through the woods bare-chested, he could feel it now. He would have preferred something longer—maybe a sweater—but one of Jones's spare work shirts from the trunk would have to do for now.

"How's the arm?" Harper asked.

"It hurts like fuck, Sarge," Beckard said. It was the only thing he had said in the last few minutes that wasn't a complete fabrication. "Jones, step on it, man. I'm dying back here."

Jones chuckled behind the wheel. "I'm already going seventy. Any faster and you might end up in the woods again, pal."

"Where did the dog go after it attacked you?" Harper asked.

"I have no friggin' idea, Sarge," Beckard said. "I was too busy running for my life."

"It wasn't hers? The dog?"

"I don't think so. I'd remember a dog in the backseat of the Ford."

"So where'd it come from?"

Beckard shrugged. "It looked wild."

"Rabies?" Jones said, still with that stupid grin on his face.

"God, I hope not," Beckard said, and played along by frowning at the suggestion he might have contracted rabies from the dog bite.

Bite? That was a mauling.

"Well, was it foaming at the mouth?" Jones asked.

"It was too dark," Beckard said. "I couldn't see shit. And, like I said, I was too busy trying to stay one step ahead of the crazy bitch."

Jones laughed again. "Some night."

"No kidding."

Harper didn't join in, and his face remained stoic. The veteran trooper was one of the more well-liked supervisors among the noncommissioned personnel at the state police. Personally, Beckard had never had any real uses for the man, and he assumed Harper would say the same thing about him, if asked. Of course, Beckard liked to think he could have won the older man over if they'd had more shifts together.

Ifs and asses don't grow on grasses.

"I called the lieutenant," Harper was saying. "Had to wake him up, but since no one's dead—yet—he's going to let us handle it until tomorrow morning when he comes in. So you have that long to get your story straight."

"Yes, sir," Beckard said. Then, because he knew Harper expected it, "But there's nothing to get straight, Sarge. I told you the whole story. All of it."

Harper nodded but said nothing. He looked out the front windshield at the other Crown Vic driving further up the road in front of them. Allie was in the backseat of the other vehicle right now. Beckard wondered if she was doing her song and dance at the moment, trying to convince the occupants of the other car the way he was in this one. She had a lot of work ahead of her, because he was pretty sure he had been mostly successful. At least with Jones. Harper, on the other hand…

Beckard was buoyed by one fact: Harper may be suspicious (*Great instincts, asshole*), but he didn't have any solid proof that Beckard was lying. He had been careful to tailor his story to match the evidence the other troopers would have found by now. His truck, the shotgun, and Allie's Ford. There wasn't a third vehicle at the crash site, so Beckard still had no idea where the hell those hunters had come from.

There were just the kids back at the cabin to worry about. The two live ones, anyway. For the life of him, Beckard couldn't figure out why they hadn't called the cops yet. All it would take was one phone call to 911 and his ass was cooked. He figured it probably had something to do with Allie. Did she say something to them? Convince them to hold off calling the cops?

I killed her sister and their friends. Maybe they agreed to let her hunt me down.

Crazy kids and their blood vendettas.

He might have chuckled softly to himself, because Harper glanced up at the rearview mirror for a brief second. "You say something?"

"Did anyone call 911?" Beckard asked.

"What do you mean?"

"Maybe someone heard all the shooting in the woods. That shotgun made a hell of a ruckus. Or maybe someone saw the cars on the side of the road?"

"We didn't get any calls." He turned almost completely around in his seat so he could look back at Beckard. "Why didn't *you* call? What happened to your cell phone?"

"I lost it in the crash. She must have tossed it before she came after me to finish the job."

Harper stared at him in silence for a moment.

"What's on your mind, Sarge?" Beckard said. He wanted to add, *Come right out and say it to my face, motherfucker.* But he said instead, "If you wanna ask me something, I'm an open book, Sarge. Besides, why would I lie? By morning, you'll be able to confirm everything I've told you, anyway."

"What's one woman doing out here in the middle of no-where, driving around with a shotgun? She doesn't live around here. Her ID says she's from Los Angeles."

Beckard shrugged. "You'll have to ask her. I just know what happened and that I'm lucky to be alive."

The trooper nodded, though Beckard knew the man was far from convinced. He turned back around, then unclipped his radio and keyed it. "Come in, Stevens."

"Stevens here," a male voice answered. Stevens was the driver of the other Crown Vic.

"Station's coming up. Take the woman to processing and then straight into one of the interrogation rooms. No one goes to see her or asks her any questions without my permission, understand?"

"Yes, sir," Stevens said.

Shit. He's going to talk to her himself.

Beckard fidgeted in his seat. Even though he wasn't re-strained, he now understood the helpless feeling that came with sitting in the back of a moving police cruiser. The backseat was claustrophobic and suffocating.

"Jones," Beckard said, "can you please drive faster? I'm dying back here."

Jones looked over at Harper for permission, but the sergeant shook his head.

Beckard gritted his teeth.

*Mother*fucker.

He sat back and concentrated on the back of Harper's head on the other side of the partition. Harper had a bit of a bald spot that wasn't apparent from the front, and Beckard wondered how hard he'd have to push to get a knife through the man's skull. The more he zeroed in on Harper's head, the more the pain faded into the background...

HE MUST HAVE dozed off during the rest of the ride to the hospital. By the time he opened his eyes to the dull backseat ceiling light shining in his face, the car had stopped and doors were slamming shut up front. Jones helped him out of the Crown Vic while Harper went on ahead to take care of the paperwork.

"You don't look so hot," Jones said.

Beckard grunted. "I was shotgunned, chased through the woods, got my nose broken, and a wild dog tried to maul my arm off. I'm peachy."

Jones chuckled. "How was Rita's, by the way?"

"I dunno. I spent most of the night trying to pick up Sarah."

"The new waitress?"

"Uh huh."

"She's hot."

"Why you think I was trying to pick her up?"

"Say no more. You get anywhere?"

"I said 'tried,' didn't I?"

"Ha ha," Jones said. "It wasn't your night, was it?"

"That's the understatement of the century, Jones. I don't think it's been my year."

"Yeah, well, night's still young."

That's what I'm counting on, he thought, but said instead, "Lord help me."

A nurse came outside with a wheelchair before they reached the lobby. Beckard sat down gratefully and was pushed inside.

The hospital was a one-floor building, just big enough to support the two closest towns along the highway. It had everything he needed, but Beckard was more concerned about its proximity to the state police station about twenty minutes, give or take, further down the road. Allie would be there right now and soon, Harper would be joining her.

Harper.

The man was trouble. Maybe even more than Allie, because people would actually believe him, whereas Allie was a stranger. Worse, a vigilante. Cops hated vigilantes, especially ones brandishing shotguns and trying to shoot one of their own. Law-enforcement types tended to demand evidence before you could whack someone.

But Harper. If he believed her, if he decided not to wait until morning when the lieutenant came in to start the investigation, then Beckard was screwed.

Shit.

He had a lot of time to think about what to do, how to handle Harper and Allie, while waiting for the doctor on call. When the doctor finally showed up at his room, Beckard was disappointed to see she was a brunette. Pretty enough, but a bit on the short side and maybe ten years too old. Way out of his range.

She gave him a cursory look before going to work unwrapping the gauze dressing around his arm that the troopers had put on him back in the woods. "Looks like you had yourself some night, trooper."

"Tell me about it," Beckard said. "Can I get something for the pain, doc? I'm really suffering here."

"What's worse, the nose, the arm, or the side?"

"I can't pick just one, doc. They all hurt like a sonofabitch."

"I need to know what I'm dealing with first." She swung a magnifying lamp over to get a better look at his arm. "Looks like you have extensive muscle and tendon damage. That's the bad news."

"You mean there's good news?"

"It didn't reach the bone."

"It feels like my arm's about to fall off."

"I bet. What did you do to it?"

"What? The dog?"

"Yes."

"Nothing. It was a wild dog."

Like Harper, she didn't look like she believed him. "Did they catch it? We need to find out if it's been immunized in case of rabies."

"Good luck with that," Beckard said. "It ran off into the woods. Like I said. Wild dog, doc."

"Dogs rarely bite people for no reason," the doctor said doubtfully.

"I don't know what to tell ya," Beckard said with a shrug. "This one did. I didn't do a damn thing to it."

"Uh huh."

Sonofabitch. I must be losing it. Can't even convince a tired doctor.

Before the woman could grill him some more, Jones appeared at the open door and leaned in. "He gonna play the piano again, doc?"

"You play the piano?" the doctor asked Beckard.

He shook his head. "He's just messing around."

"Hunh," she said.

"Where's Harper?" Beckard asked Jones.

"Robbins picked him up a few minutes ago," the other trooper said.

"He went home?"

"Back to the station."

Of course he did.

"He's hot to interrogate the woman," Jones continued, then made a gun with his finger and "shot" Beckard. "He's probably really interested in how a 120-pound woman got the jump on you. Hell, we all are."

"I told you, the crash knocked me out," Beckard said, but he was already thinking, *Harper, you motherfucker.* He said to Jones, "Once the doc knits me back up, can you give me a ride back home? I'm exhausted, man."

"You don't wanna stay the night?"

"Do I have to?" Beckard asked the doctor.

"You mean you don't *want* to stay?" she said, looking surprised.

"Not if I don't have to."

"You're pretty bad off, trooper. I wouldn't be doing my job if I didn't insist you spend the night."

"But I don't have to…"

She shook her head. He had expected more of a fight, but apparently the woman couldn't care less if he dropped dead soon. That should have made him a bit peeved, but Beckard was instead impressed with her indifference.

"I can't make you stay," she said. "You'll have to sign forms saying that you're refusing medical treatment."

"You're crazy, man," Jones said from the door.

"Give me the papers to sign," Beckard said to the doctor.

She shrugged. "Your funeral."

"Until then, can you at least make sure I don't bleed to death before I step out of this place?"

"I'll see what I can do," she said.

He grinned. He was really starting to like her. Maybe he could even overlook her height and age…

"HELL OF A night, huh?" Jones said when they were back on the highway again. "At least you got to go to Rita's. I might stop in after work, see if Sarah's still there. Wanna come and take a second swing at the prize?"

"I think I'm done with Rita's for a while," Beckard said.

"Oh, come on, don't be such a baby," Jones laughed. "One dog bite and some buckshot, and you're crying like a little girl."

"That damn mutt almost took my entire arm off, man."

"Waaah," Jones said, mimicking a baby crying.

Beckard smiled. He liked Jones. They had known each other since their cadet days, so he wasn't really looking forward to doing this. He had his knife, which Jones had given back to him after the hospital, but knives were always tricky. Besides, there was another, better option.

Now sitting in the front passenger seat, Beckard reached over and pulled out Jones's gun from its holster.

"What the fuck you doing?" Jones said, his eyes widening. He might have grabbed for the gun back if both his hands weren't on the steering wheel.

"Sorry," Beckard said, shoving the Glock against Jones's temple. "Pull over to the shoulder."

Jones swallowed and did as he was told.

"Turn off the lights," Beckard said.

Jones did. Not that he really needed to. The highway was always empty this time of the morning. It would be a few more hours before the truckers started coming through in a constant stream. For now, there wasn't another vehicle in either direction, leaving the headlights of the Crown Vic a lonely pool of bright lights in a sea of black nothing.

It was perfect.

"What are you doing, man?" Jones asked.

The trooper looked genuinely scared, which told Beckard he hadn't seen the way Beckard's right hand was shaking. Just the effort of holding the gun up made him wince, every sensitive muscle that the dog's teeth had torn through earlier rippling mercilessly.

"Out of the car," Beckard said.

He opened the passenger-side door and climbed out, secretly grimacing when Jones couldn't see him, and quickly changed the gun to his left hand. Beckard was right-handed like most of the world's population, and if he had to shoot the cop from long distance—and at this point, long-distance was anything over a foot—he didn't like his chances.

Jones climbed out of the other side and stared at him across the roof. "What are you doing, Beckard? What the *fuck* are you doing, man?"

Beckard didn't answer him. He circled around the hood of the squad car instead before saying, "Assume the position."

"What?"

"Assume the fucking position!"

Jones did, facing his driver-side door and spreading his legs before putting his arms behind his head.

"Don't fuck with me!" Beckard shouted. He wasn't worried about being overheard. They might as well be the only two living souls in the universe, given the emptiness around them at the moment.

Jones reluctantly laced his fingers together. "What now?"

"Sorry, buddy," Beckard said. "I always liked you."

"What are you—" Jones started to say, but never finished because Beckard shoved the Glock against the back of trooper's head and pulled the trigger.

It was hard to miss from that kind of range, even left-handed.

CHAPTER 17

SHE DIDN'T SAY a word between the time they threw her into the police car, during the long drive to the police station, and when they booked her before eventually putting her into an interrogation room in the back of a long hallway. There, they handcuffed her right wrist to a steel ring at the edge of the table. The room was sparse and there were no recording devices she could see, or even one of those one-way mirrors where someone could watch her from a connected room.

Allie didn't say anything, because they didn't ask her anything.

After about five minutes, a female trooper named Tanner finally showed up to check her for injuries. Tanner jotted down notes on a cheap notepad, indicating her bruised side and the dry blood she had forgotten to completely wipe from around her mouth. Allie made sure the trooper saw the additional bruising along her wrists and ankles from the duct tape. She kept waiting for Tanner to ask a question, but the woman never did.

Tanner left twenty minutes later, but not before handcuffing her back to the table. She sat in silence and resumed waiting.

It was cold inside the small room, and very quiet. The building had been mostly empty when they brought her in, which wasn't surprising, given where she was and the time of day. It wasn't as if these people saw a lot of crimes in their jurisdiction—at least, not since the Roadside Killer "retired."

She knew from her trips to the area that law enforcement in the surrounding two counties spent most of their time dealing with highway accidents and writing tickets, and you didn't need a lot of manpower for that between midnight and early morning. She had counted less than ten people in the entire building, and most of them looked bored. There wasn't the buzz resulting from the action in the woods that she had expected, which surprised her a bit.

Allie didn't know when she laid her head down on the table, but she didn't open her eyes again until the door *clicked* open and one of the troopers, an older man with blond hair, stepped inside.

"Allie Krycek," the man said.

She waited for him to continue, but he didn't. Instead, he sat down across the table from her, then opened a folder with her name on the label and began flipping through it. Like the other cops in the building, he looked ready to go home and get some sleep.

What's it going to take to get these people excited?

"How are you?" he asked. His nametag read: "Sgt. Harper."

"Is that a rhetorical question?"

He looked up and smiled. "I genuinely want to know how you are right now, Allie. May I call you Allie?"

"Why not."

"Before we start, do you need immediate medical attention? Do you need me to take you to a hospital? I want to make sure you're all right to continue."

"I'm fine," she lied.

The truth was, her ribs were killing her, but at the moment she needed to talk to this man more than she needed to see a doctor. The idea of Beckard still running around out there made her grind her teeth.

"Where is he?" she asked.

"What about your ribs?" Harper asked, ignoring her question. "You told Corporal Tanner they were broken. Are you sure you don't need a doctor to look at them?"

"I'll live for now. Where is he?" she asked again.

"Who?"

"Beckard. If that's his real name."

Harper nodded. "That's his real name."

"What did he tell you?"

Harper didn't answer right away. He went back to flipping through the papers in front of him in silence for a moment. He was in his early forties, and out here she guessed the girls probably called someone with his looks handsome, though back in L.A. he would be invisible on the streets.

"That you're dangerous," Harper said finally.

He closed the folder and put his hands over it, then looked across at her with a measured stare that she couldn't decide if it was an attempt at intimidation or…something else. She could easily picture him in an old Western, the aw-shucks sheriff who was smarter than the country bumpkin vibe he gave off.

Or she could have been misreading him completely.

"He's lying," Allie said.

"Trooper Beckard?"

"Yes."

"I didn't tell you what he said."

"It doesn't matter. He's lying. And I can prove it."

"How?"

"There's a cabin in the woods…"

Harper smiled.

"What?" she said, unable to hide her annoyance.

"It's an old trooper joke," Harper said. "A cabin in the woods invariably comes up during an investigation out here." He waved it off. "Sorry. Go on…"

"There is a *cabin in the woods*," she continued, "where you'll find all the evidence you'll need that Beckard is lying through his teeth. Your fellow trooper left behind four bodies, but he also made the mistake of leaving behind two eyewitnesses. And a dog."

"A dog?"

"Beckard killed its owner."

"You said there are four bodies out there? At this cabin?"

"Yes."

The police sergeant leaned back in his chair. He had calm eyes, and they hadn't left her face the entire time. Now, he seemed to be really peering at her, and for just a moment she was afraid the man could stare right into her soul.

"And you said there are eyewitnesses?" Harper asked.

"Two of them."

"In this cabin in the woods."

"Correct."

"So why haven't we heard from them?"

"Because I told them not to call 911 until sunrise."

"And why did you do that?"

"I needed the time to kill Beckard first."

She expected a bigger reaction, but Harper simply lifted both eyebrows as if to say, *"Hunh."*

"That's it?" she said.

"Hmm?"

"I just told you I wanted to kill one of your troopers, and all you do is raise your eyebrows?"

"I don't like Beckard, either," Harper said. "The guy rubs me the wrong way. Whenever I meet him, like tonight, I always think he's hiding something. That he's doing something he doesn't want me to know. Doesn't want anyone to know." The trooper shrugged again. "Where is this cabin in the woods?"

"You actually believe me…"

"Can't hurt to check."

"I don't know the exact location, but it's not far from the crash site. Maybe a mile northwest."

"A cabin one mile northwest from the crash site?"

"I think so. I'm not sure. It was dark, and I was mostly just stumbling around following his blood trail."

"Beckard's."

"Yes."

"After you shotgunned him."

"Yes."

"Hunh." Harper nodded and seemed to drift off momentarily.

"What?" she prompted.

"There are some good hunting grounds just beyond the crash site," Harper said. "A lot of hunters have blinds out there. The ones with a lot of money have cabins."

"This one wasn't that small. Two bedrooms and a bath."

"Not many of those around…"

"You actually believe me."

She couldn't hide her surprise. She was sure Beckard would have poisoned the well by now. Not just with Harper, but the entire state police in the hour or so since her arrest. He had done a masterful job convincing the college kids back at the cabin, and he didn't even know them. These were his people, his colleagues.

And yet here was Harper nodding at her. "I believe that you believe it, Allie."

It was probably just her imagination, but her ribs seemed to have stopped hurting and she was having less trouble breathing. Even the cold in the room seemed to have faded and the handcuff around her right wrist not quite as biting.

"What now?" she asked Harper.

He glanced at his watch. "The lieutenant doesn't get up for another three hours, and he won't be in for another five. I'm just the night supervisor, so it's not my call to make—"

"Beckard is the Roadside Killer," Allie said.

Now *that* got the response she was hoping for.

"What are you talking about?" Harper asked.

"Beckard. He's the Roadside Killer."

"The Roadside Killer retired. He hasn't been active in seven years."

"You're wrong. He never stopped. He just got more careful." She leaned forward, staring Harper in the eyes, willing him to see and *believe* her. "He's one of you, don't you get it? He's a cop. He didn't retire to Mexico or Cabo. He just adapted. He got smarter. He's been working the highway, killing all this time, and you don't even know it."

"But you did," Harper said.

"Yes."

"CID closed the case five years ago. Even the feds stopped pursuing clues. Are you saying you managed to do something, by yourself, that both of those organizations couldn't with all their manpower?"

"Yes."

"How?"

"Because I had no choice."

"Meaning?"

"He killed my little sister ten years ago," Allie said. "For you, the state police and the feds, it was a job. To me, it was god-damn personal."

HARPER LEFT TWENTY minutes later, and Allie did her best to temper her growing excitement. The state police sergeant had believed her.

He had believed her!

She hadn't anticipated finding an ally out here, especially this late in the game. She was always convinced it was going to be a solo job; her against the world. The authorities would never believe her because she didn't have a name or a face or anything that would constitute "evidence." She had a gut feeling, anecdotes, piles of police reports and newspaper clippings, and endless nights to put them all together. All those killings that were supposed to be random, that she knew weren't. He had gotten smarter, craftier, and was spreading out his murders beyond his usual hunting ground, even leaving the state once or twice.

But it was him. She knew it was him. She *felt* it.

And now Harper was on his way to the cabin. Even if he never found it, soon Wade would call 911 and it would be over for Beckard. He had to know that, didn't he? Sooner or later, his lies would unravel and he would have to run.

So was that what he was doing now? Running?

If he was smart, anyway.

Harper had told her Beckard was taken to the hospital, then later driven home by one of the troopers. The sergeant had been smart about it; he wouldn't contact Beckard until he found the cabin and talked to Wade and Rachel. When they had all the evidence they needed, they would swoop in and take Beckard. But only then.

"It's tricky," Harper had said. "He's one of us. If we move on him now, and it turns out you're lying to me—"

"I'm not," she had interrupted.

"*If* it turns out you're lying," Harper had continued, "my career is DOA. You understand, right? I can't move on him yet, not without corroboration from these college kids."

She had nodded grudgingly. Harper had his livelihood to think about, and to just take the word of a woman who had been caught carrying a shotgun around in the woods, who had already admitted to trying to kill one of his troopers…

Yeah, she didn't blame him. She would have done the exact same thing in his shoes.

Of course, none of that made waiting in the interrogation room after he left any easier. She also swore the temperature had started dropping again. Harper had believed enough of what she had told him to take off the handcuffs, which allowed her to get up and walk around to fight against the growing chill.

She paced back and forth, walking the entire length of the room at least a dozen times in as many minutes. They had taken her watch when they processed her, so she didn't know what time it was. When he was in here, Harper had told her his lieutenant wasn't going to wake up for another three hours. Six in the morning, she guessed. Maybe seven, if the higher-ranked trooper was a late riser.

And Harper had just left thirty minutes ago—or had it been an hour now?

Time had a way of slipping by when all you had was gray concrete to stare at. Suddenly she wished there was a two-way mirror across from her so she could get someone's attention. The door remained locked from the other side, and she couldn't see anyone in the hallway through the security window. When she tried the door, it wouldn't budge. She wondered if she could ram it open with her shoulders, but it felt too solid, and she wasn't sure she could risk it with her broken ribs. Besides, although she couldn't see a guard outside, that didn't mean there wasn't one further up the hallway.

The quiet inside and outside the room was unsettling. The entire building had seemed asleep when she first showed up, but it was downright dead at the moment.

And she was tired. So tired.

Maybe it was the ribs. Or the bruised skin around her wrists and ankles. She had also gained a couple of extra bumps when the troopers tackled her back at the crash site, because apparently the rest of her body hadn't been hurting enough.

Gee, thanks for that, guys.

With nothing to do and no one to talk to, she continued pacing the room, willing Harper to hurry up and reach the cabin.

If he could find it. There was no guarantee of that, either, especially at night. She remembered being led out of the woods in the police cruiser and the seemingly endless walls of silent trees standing at sentry on both sides of the highway.

Podunk country. What did you expect?

The *click* of the door opening snapped her back. She was on the other side of the table, looking across the room.

"Did you find the cabin?" Allie asked.

"The cabin?" he said, pushing the door open and standing in the open frame with a gun in his fist.

Beckard.

He looked like shit. Worse than shit, really.

His face was purple and black, with a big Band-Aid over the bridge of his broken nose so that when he talked, his voice sounded slightly muffled. His right hand was bundled up in thick gauze tape and hung loosely at his side like a useless sack of meat. Which explained why he was using his left hand to hold the gun. He was favoring his right side, where she had put buckshot through him last night, as he stood there looking in at her.

Allie wondered what the chances were that he was not ambi-dextrous. It was hard to shoot a gun straight, and even harder to shoot a gun with your weak hand. That same ex-cop had taught her that. Even this close, it might be worth taking the chance to test his accuracy—

He must have seen the spark of a plan forming in her eyes, because he smiled. "I'd like to take you with me, but I'm not against shooting you and starting over. Understand?"

"You shoot me, and everyone will hear the gunshot."

He shrugged. "You've been a thorn in my side all night,

missy. At this point, if I can't take you with me, I'm just gonna end it now and call it a career. It's been one hell of a ride already. Ten years. Brett Favre wishes he had my winning streak."

"Bullshit."

"You think so? Try me, then."

She stared into those dark, soulless eyes and knew he meant it. He would die here if he had to, if it meant taking her with him.

Remember, he's a psychopath.

She nodded. "All right. So now what?"

He reached behind his back (she could see him wincing with the effort and thought, *Hurts, asshole?*) and brought back a pair of handcuffs and tossed it onto the table. It skidded across the metal surface and over to her.

"Remember," he said, "we both get out of here alive, or neither one of us does. Frankly, I don't give a shit anymore."

CHAPTER 18

THE STATE POLICE had its own stretch of land just off the main highway, with the closest town more than ten miles further down the road. The unremarkable one-floor building housed fifty or so troopers that worked the three shifts and would have been easily missed if not for the brightly-lit parking lot and spotlights along the outer walls.

Beckard knew the building intimately, including where to enter without being seen and how to leave in the same manner. He also knew that Allie was being kept inside the interrogation room in the back of the hallway, though he was surprised by the lack of a guard outside her door. Alarms went off inside his head and Beckard fully expected some kind of trap to be sprung. He stood in the narrow passageway for a good two, maybe three minutes with the Glock in his hand, listening and waiting for his fellow troopers to converge on him.

But they never did.

Finally, he decided there was no trap and went to collect Allie.

He marched her at gunpoint to the same side door he had used to enter unnoticed. The door was accessible by an access panel that he, of course, knew the code to. As she moved quietly in front of him, Beckard could picture her eyes shifting, looking for a way out—something, *anything*—even if he could only see the back of her head. Maybe a few hours weren't enough to know a person, but Beckard felt as if he knew this woman intimately.

She's just my type, too.

"Faster," he grunted. "Remember. If I don't get out of here, you don't get out of here. If you think I won't shoot you purely out of spite, you're dead wrong."

"I know you will," she said.

It felt as if they were the only two people moving and talking in the entire place, their voices and footsteps echoing off the hallway walls. Beckard rarely worked the skeleton shift, but it was a cemetery in here despite all the excitement just a few hours ago.

"Oh yeah?" he said.

"I've studied you," Allie said. Her voice was calm, measured. *She's got ice in her veins, this one.*

"Have you now?" he said.

"Yes."

"And what did you find out?"

"Besides the fact you're a sadistic sonofabitch with, in all likelihood, a small dick?"

He chuckled. "Besides that."

"You're going to lose."

"To you?"

"Yes."

"Keep dreaming."

"You want to know why?"

"Sure, why not."

"Because you won't be able to help yourself. It's in your nature. You're a loser."

She's baiting you. Don't fall for it.

"Keep moving," he said.

It took a lot of effort not to bash in the back of her head with the Glock. He didn't do it because he wanted to enjoy her later; that, and he was afraid moving that quickly might send him collapsing to the floor from pure exhaustion. Because every inch of his body was on fire at this very moment.

He took out the bottle of painkillers and shook out two, then swallowed them in one gulp. Beckard kept the gun in front of him so that if anyone saw him from behind, they wouldn't see he had the weapon out. Of course, if anyone caught him in the hallway with her, he was dead in the water anyway.

They turned another corner and finally reached the side door.

"Outside," Beckard said.

She pushed the door open and stepped out into the chilly night. It was still pitch-black outside except for a floodlight above the side door that lit up the both of them. Her hands were still handcuffed, so Beckard hurried in front of her, making sure she could see the Glock in his hand the entire time. An aimed weapon, he had found from past escapades, was a stronger deterrent than vocal threats.

He opened the back door of Jones's police cruiser. "Inside."

She stared into the backseat and frowned. "Is he dead?"

"Shut up and get inside," he hissed.

She climbed in and he slammed the door behind her. The rear doors didn't have levers on the interior to open with and the windows didn't roll down (that was the point of stashing prisoners back there, after all). He knew he had her imprisoned as he circled the front hood, holstered the handgun, and slipped into the driver's seat.

Beckard started the car and pulled away from the building, heading toward the back where there were fewer lights and chances of people. The last thing he needed now was to stumble across a couple of troopers smoking out front.

He picked up the familiar back trail and turned left toward the highway just as a semi blasted up the road, bright headlights spilling across them for a brief second. The Crown Vic slid back onto the smooth highway as he turned right.

He glanced up at the rearview mirror, at Allie in the semi-darkness behind the partition. She was looking down at something on the floor. That "something" would be Jones. Dead, with a bullet hole in the back of his head.

"Ignore the body," Beckard said. "Where we're going, it's going to be the least of your worries."

She met his eyes in the mirror. He expected to see fear, but instead there was a resoluteness, a grim determination that bothered him. Beckard didn't let her see it, though—or at least, he didn't think he had—and grinned back at her instead. It took quick thinking, but he (probably) succeeded.

"Allie Krycek," he said, letting her name roll off his tongue. Yes, he liked the sound of it. "You came all the way out here just for me, huh? Ever since I took your sister what, ten years ago? I'm flattered. Really. Tell me, how much of your life did you spend just thinking about me?"

"Ten years," she said.

Her voice was calm. Again, that bothered him, but Beckard

played it off.

"Ten years," he repeated. "Like I said, I'm flattered. Tell me something: Was this how you thought it would go down?"

"No."

"You thought it'd be easier, didn't you? Admit it."

She didn't respond.

"I liked your sister," he said. "She was sweet."

There. He saw a reaction. The hardness gave way to vulnerability, if just for a split second.

The sister's the Achilles heel. I can work with that.

"She was soft," he continued. "I like them soft. She cried a lot, but then, they all did, so she wasn't special in that respect. Do you want me to show you where I played with her? Before I gave her back to the highway?"

She didn't say a word, but her face gave it all away. He could see it in the way she was looking at him—trying to figure out how to get to him the way he had gotten to her. He knew exactly what she was thinking.

"We're going to have a lot of fun," he smiled. "Hell, when we're done, you might not want to ever leave. Wouldn't that be something?"

More silence, but her eyes continued to dart left and right. They were just the barest of movements, searching, but she couldn't hide it from him.

"You'll open up," he said. "It's just a matter of time. I usually don't spend more than twenty-four hours with my friends, but you…I think I might make an exception for you, Allie Krycek."

HE HAD IT all planned out. The location. The timing. He had even carved out an extra day or two in a best-case scenario, in case her name didn't show up on the wires as a missing person right away. If he was lucky, no one would be expecting her. After all, not every traveler was a planner. Some of the girls he'd taken in the past weren't identified for months afterward because, simply, no one knew they had taken off on a cross-country trip.

Of course, Allie Krycek wasn't your ordinary traveler. She wasn't a traveler at all.

Come into my web, said the spider to the fly…

He could tell just by sneaking a look at her in the backseat of the cruiser, using the rearview mirror, that she was preparing herself for what was coming. As if she had any clue. He had evolved since the last time he met a Krycek.

Her face was partially lit by moonlight, and she didn't say a word as he turned off the highway and drove into an unmarked part of the woods. The ground under them immediately became uneven, and he grunted a couple of times when the jostling sent some stabbing pains through his side.

Maybe this wasn't such a good idea…

It was still pitch-black outside, and the combination of night and densely packed trees all around them made for dangerous traveling companions. Fortunately, the Crown Vic had a strong pair of headlights that allowed him to see where he was going. Even so, he drove slowly. This was a part of the country he was familiar with, but he'd never been here at night before.

A part of him knew this was a bad idea. There were going to be police cars all over the highway by morning and even more by afternoon. He knew Harper had been talking to her, and the sergeant might even have believed some of it. Not that it mattered; sooner or later, they would find out that Jones was missing. Even if they couldn't find the body, Harper would be able to put two and two together easily enough.

Once they realized he had taken Allie too, they would mobilize everyone to look for him. All the shifts. They might even call in the feds again, though not so early on. Hell, depending on how much Allie had told Harper, they probably already knew he was the Roadside Killer. All of it led to the same thing: A manhunt.

So be it. I've had a good run.

"Revenge," he said, looking at the rearview mirror.

Her face dipped in and out of patches of darkness, depending on how thick and tall the walls of trees around them were. There was just enough occasional light for him to see her staring back at him silently.

"I've been wondering why Wade and Rachel haven't called 911 yet. You told them not to, didn't you? Convinced them somehow. Well, it probably wasn't too hard after what I did to Donnie and Sabrina."

He searched for the telltale signs that he was right—or at least close—but saw nothing on her face to confirm it.

"I don't blame them. I don't blame you, either. You spent ten years looking for me. Studying me. You're obsessed. I know a little bit about that, too. How long have you been setting this whole thing up? How long were you out there, driving back and forth, waiting for me to notice you? A week? Two weeks? Months? It must have been months."

The only response was her body swaying slightly from side to side in tune with the car's motions.

"And that fancy driving you did back there, that's some pro stuff. Someone taught you tactical driving, didn't they?"

Did she just blink, or was that his imagination?

"Spent a lot of money, too, I bet. A lot of time and effort went into this, I can tell. You didn't even go to the cops with what you knew. Or thought you knew. I'm guessing you didn't have anything concrete, but you had a lot of guesses. A lot of maybes. Then, of course, there was that shotgun in the trunk."

She might have smirked. Or was that just the movement of the car again?

"But your biggest mistake so far? You should have let the college kids call 911. Instead, you dropped the ball. Call it overconfidence. Either way, it's going to cost you."

"You think so?" she said.

Finally.

He smiled. "Who's the one sitting in the backseat of a police cruiser?"

"We'll see."

"You got a plan? I know you have a plan."

She clammed up again.

"Of course you do. It better be a good one, cause this might just be the last time you get to breathe fresh air."

He slowed down before easing off the dirt road and onto a narrow hiking lane. Overgrown grass slapped at the sides and brush scraped against the undercarriage of the cruiser. He dropped the speed to ten miles per hour until he was moving almost at a crawl. It couldn't be helped; this part of the wood, even more so than the previous stretch, was potentially treacherous.

"I admire your persistence," he said. "Ten years. Of course, you could say I've been doing this for just as long. So we have that in common."

He expected (wanted) the back-and-forth to continue, but she apparently decided not to respond to his latest volley.

"Except I've been far more successful," he grinned.

Nothing.

"What did you do while you were preparing for this? Secretary? Lawyer? You look like a lawyer. You definitely worked in an office, I know that for a fact."

She was looking out the window at the passing trees.

"Fine. Be boring."

He drove on in silence for a few more minutes before making a final turn and coming to a complete stop in the middle of a rough clearing. He put the Crown Vic into park and turned around in his seat.

She was staring back at him.

"Is it everything you thought it would be?" he asked.

She looked past him for a moment. "What am I looking at? Your invisible lair?"

"Look closer."

"I am."

"Closer."

"You're delusional," she said. "There's nothing there."

"Oh, but there is," he said, beaming now. "Home sweet home. The best part? They'll never find you out here, and I'll be able to play with you for as long as I want, however I want. Won't that be nice? Well, for one of us, anyway…"

CHAPTER 19

IF YOU GO *down there, you'll never come back up.*

The problem was doing something to stop it from happening. Even if Harper believed her and talked to the kids back at the cabin, he'd still have to find where Beckard took her first. She didn't know the area, so she didn't have a clue where they were, only that it was densely wooded, similar to where she had clashed with Beckard earlier that night.

It was some kind of backup location, she guessed. A hideout. Beckard probably always knew that sooner or later his luck would run out. Her instinct was to call this a mistake on his part—staying around in the area knowing he might be (or had already been) exposed. But the more she thought about it, maybe it wasn't such a stupid thing to do after all. Beckard would know, more than most, about the risks of staying on the road if he was being pursued by the police. He would understand the effectiveness of a statewide roadblock, especially in this part of the country, where the closest big city to get lost in was still a long way off.

Of course, there was a very real possibility he wasn't thinking straight, that the pills he was popping liberally (that he didn't think she noticed him doing) were playing tricks with his mind. Was it possible for him to overdose on painkillers? Or at least choke on them?

Not with my luck.

It was some kind of old building, about twice the size of a backyard shack, and made of brick. Its exterior had, over the years, been partially swallowed up by the woods that surrounded it, making it very easy to miss if you didn't know what you were looking for, or where exactly to look. How long had it been here? Decades and decades. Forgotten, until a psychopath in need of a place to hide showed up one day.

The entrance was behind a rusted-over black metal gate covered in vines and moss, and to get to it, Beckard had to pull down what looked like a large green and brown tarp covered in branches, leaves, and dirt. It wasn't anything natural, but some kind of makeshift hunting canvas that he had put together to camouflage the opening.

Beckard disappeared around the building for a moment before returning with a key he had apparently gone to retrieve from somewhere. He used it now to open a large padlock and swung the metal gate wide open in order to get at the wooden door on the other side. It was old and heavy, and Beckard had to put his entire body into it just to move it. She prayed he snapped his stitches and would maybe bleed to death.

No such luck, because he pushed the door open just enough to reveal bright LED lights hanging from the ceiling. She couldn't make out much of anything else from the backseat of the police cruiser where Beckard had left her. The only reason she could see what he was doing and where was because of the car's headlights.

He walked back to her now, drawing the Glock when he was almost at the car. He opened the door and motioned her out, and Allie once again wondered if he was ambidextrous, and if not, how accurate he would be shooting with his left hand.

"Find out," he said, smiling at her.

Shit.

She climbed out silently, clumsily. She had to grab onto the open door with both hands to maintain her balance because of the handcuffs.

He moved behind her and poked her in the back with the cold gun barrel before she was completely outside. "Into the abyss, Allie Krycek."

She walked toward the building, drawn to the open door and the warmth of the lights flooding outside. Against the backdrop of the darkened woods, it looked very much like an ominous entrance to someplace that was not meant for human visitation.

If you go down there, you'll never come back up.

"Found it a couple of years back," Beckard said behind her, as if he were discussing his favorite T-shirt. "I've been getting it ready ever since. You never know when you'll need a place to hide once the chickens come home to roost. And I think today qualifies."

Scarred concrete blocks on the other side of the door came into view. Someone had originally painted the walls in a lime-green color, but it had faded over the years, leaving just the natural gray behind, with a patch or streak of lime-green still holding on here and there. Cobwebs clung to the corners, and something furry scurried into her path, appearing out of the opening and disappearing into the freedom of the woods before she could get a good look at it.

"Go right in, don't be shy," Beckard said.

When she stepped inside, she understood why the shack-like building had looked small from the outside—that was because it was just an entrance. About five feet from the door was the first of many steps leading down. She counted ten in all before the stairs made a sharp right turn around a corner. Another lamp hung along the wall further down, illuminating a dirty and dust-covered landing. Allie thought she heard the *thrumming* of something from below, around the turn, but maybe it was just her own labored breathing.

"Down you go, princess," Beckard said behind her before chuckling. "Bet you've heard that before, huh?"

She didn't answer and didn't move right away.

If you go down there, you'll never come back up.

"Come on," Beckard said, poking her in the back with the gun again. "This isn't a democracy. You don't have a choice."

Every time he prodded her with the gun, her instincts were to twist around and grab for the weapon. But she needed him to be close enough to do that, and there was still the problem of the handcuffs. Those were, though, doable as long as he was *close enough.* Allie didn't have any illusions that she could take Beckard if he was at full-strength, but maybe now, at half *(maybe less)* strength, she might stand a chance—

"You'll have to be fast," he said, and she could hear the amusement in his voice.

Goddammit. How does he always know?

She took the first step down and wondered if this was what a death row inmate felt as he was being led to his end.

"It's amazing how much you look like your sister," he said between steps. "Now that I know the two of you are related, I can't look at you without seeing her. It's uncanny."

He wasn't wrong. She did look like Carmen, but only because she had made an effort to. The blonde hair and slender frame was a part of it. Allie had always been more naturally curvy than thin, but dieting and steady cardio exercises over the years had fixed that. The Krycek girls had always been tall, so that was never an issue. The green eyes, on the other hand, were contact lenses covering up her natural blues. She had become so used to them during the four months that she spent traveling back and forth between the same stretch of road, waiting for him to bite, that she hardly remembered she had them on.

She hesitated as he reached the landing, with the turn coming up.

"Don't stop now; you're almost there," he said, poking her in the back of the neck with the gun this time. The barrel was much colder than it should have been and sent shivers through her body.

She turned the corner and saw another flight of stairs. This one was shorter, with only five steps, and it led to the bottom where another lamp hanging from the ceiling revealed more of the wall's original lime-green color.

It was some kind of underground bunker. Maybe one of those old school bomb shelters.

Small, the size of a single studio apartment. There was a cot along one wall and shelves stacked with black boxes with pictures of food on them. Spare lamps hung from hooks, and the outlines of strange, bulky objects peered back at her from shadowed corners. The overwhelming stench of abandonment was suffocating.

The floor was hard and rough and absorbed the sounds of

her footsteps as she walked across it. More cobwebs dotted the ceiling, and a pair of cockroaches ran across her path and vanished into a crack along the wall. Something else moved in one of the darkened corners to her right. It was a brief scurrying noise, but Allie decided she'd rather not find out what had caused it.

"Welcome to your new home," Beckard said behind her. "Now be a good girl and stay very still."

She heard a *click!* and another large swath of the room lit up as he turned on a second LED lamp hanging along the wall.

"What now?" she asked. She couldn't tell where he was behind her exactly or how close.

"Walk to the far wall, turn around, and sit down."

She did as he instructed, turning around as she slowly sat down Indian style.

He had taken out a second pair of handcuffs and now tossed it into her lap. "Put one end around the cuffs you have on now, and the other into that," he said, pointing at a thick metal spike with a round loop at the end, jutting out of the wall a few inches to the left of her. "Don't get cute," he added with a grin. "I want to hear the sound of that lock catching."

She picked up the second pair of handcuffs and hooked one over the chain between the first handcuff, then slipped it into the spike. As a result, her arms were now suspended slightly in the air and she had to sit sideways facing the center of the room with her right shoulder pressed against the wall. She shivered slightly from the cold contact.

"You're taking this well," he said, holstering the handgun.

"Disappointed?"

"A little. I expected more of a fight."

He walked over to the cot and sat down. It creaked loudly under his weight, but he didn't seem to notice it. He was too busy pulling out a white bottle from his pocket. He shook out a couple of pills and swallowed them.

"Generic brand," he said, even though she hadn't asked, "but it works just as well. I can barely feel the pain." He stood up and flinched a bit, which led her to think he was lying about "barely" feeling the pain. "I gotta go do something. Until I come back, you be a good girl and don't go anywhere."

He started up the stairs, but stopped halfway and looked back at her.

"Oh, feel free to scream if you want." He banged his fist on the wall, producing a dull *thud* each time. "Fifties construction. They really knew how to build things back then. You could set off a nuke in here, and someone standing on the other side of the door wouldn't hear it. But hey, don't take my word for it."

He continued up, whistling to himself, his footsteps fading.

Then the grind of the heavy door against the concrete floor as it closed.

She waited…and heard the low rumbling of the Crown Vic starting up. Beckard was wrong; the bunker wasn't soundproof. Noises didn't travel freely down here from the outside world, but it was noticeable and she could feel the engine vibrating slightly along the structure.

She didn't move until everything was quiet and still again, signaling that Beckard was gone.

She turned her focus to the metal thing protruding out of the wall next to her and spent some time examining it closely. Her arms were already starting to tire from being suspended in the air. All those nights of lying in bed, dreaming up nightmare scenarios, and not one of them involved being handcuffed to a wall in an old bunker.

She didn't panic, though. Allie had come too far to start doing that now.

Ten years of research, six years of training, and three years of getting ready for this moment...

She jingled the handcuffs and took a breath.

It was going to hurt.

Oh, who was she kidding?

It was going to hurt *a lot*.

CHAPTER 20

HE ALWAYS KNEW it would end one day, and ten years was a hell of a good run. He would have preferred twenty, but you couldn't really go wrong with a nice solid decade of work.

So he was fully prepared when that time came. Finding the bunker had been a nice stroke of luck, thanks to some city campers that had gone missing two years ago. He had stumbled across the place during the search for those dummies. There were times when he considered using it as part of his hunts, but he had always resisted. He was glad he had.

He couldn't go back to his apartment. By now, Harper would have talked to those college kids at the cabin and there would be an all-points bulletin out on him. That was a bummer, because it meant his entire life was torched. Everything that was Thomas Beckard would be placed under a microscope, and everything he owned gone through with a fine-tooth comb.

Fortunately, he had other things even the state police wouldn't be able to get to until later in the day.

It was still dark out when he turned back onto the highway and drove to his destination. It took him half an hour to get there, but the ride was pleasant enough without Jones's body stinking up the interior of the Crown Vic.

He parked in front of the regional bank and climbed out. He would have liked to go further, put more distance from the shelter, but the risk of being spotted on the highway was too great.

Beckard withdrew as much money as he could from the ATM and didn't bother to hide his face from the camera. He probably had a full day before his former comrades got a warrant to freeze his assets, including his bank accounts, so what he pocketed now would likely be it. He wished he'd had the foresight to stash away cash back at the hideout, but it wasn't as if he had a lot of money *to* put away. The state police didn't exactly pay a king's ransom.

Inside the gas station, the pimple-faced kid behind the counter looked up from his smartphone when Beckard entered. The teenager did a double take at the sight of him and Beckard grinned back. He knew he didn't look his usual handsome self, but that was one hell of a reaction.

"Hey," Beckard said. "Slow night, huh?"

"Yeah," the kid said. The nametag over his left breast pocket read: "Ben."

Beckard could see the kid trying not to stare as he walked up the aisle and picked up the things he needed. By the time he was done, he had grabbed two baskets and Ben was stuffing the items into three large bags.

"You going camping or something?" Ben asked.

"Not quite," Beckard said. "How much I owe ya?"

Ben rang him up and Beckard paid with one of his credit cards. The plastics, like the bank accounts, were going to be next to useless soon anyway, and there was no harm in letting Harper know he was still around the area at—what time was it? Five in the morning.

Geez. Time flies when you're killing people.

"You need help with those?" Ben asked, looking at the bags Beckard was grabbing off the counter.

"Nah, I got it," Beckard said, giving the kid another grin. He got a kick out of Ben trying his best not to stare. "See you around, Ben."

"Yeah, you too."

Beckard tossed the bags into the backseat of the squad car, then climbed in and drove off. It would probably be later in the day until Harper or one of the other troopers got around to canvassing the area and showed his picture to the locals. By then, Ben would probably be at home since he clearly worked the graveyard shift.

Not that any of it mattered. Thomas Beckard's life was over. The faster he accepted that, the quicker he could deal with the fallout. All he had to do was outlast the coming storm.

Yeah, that's the ticket.

If all else failed, well, he'd already gotten away with it for ten years. Hell, he didn't think he'd last more than a couple of months when he first started this, so the last ten years was all gravy. When he told himself that, it made his decision to stay and hide much easier to stomach. Of course, he could just be fooling himself, but Beckard was feeling too good to care at the moment.

It's the pills. I'm not thinking straight. I should be fleeing this place. Right now.

But I'm not.

Why?

He pulled the bottle out of his pocket and opened it with one hand, shook out two more pills, and swallowed them.

Now, where was he?

He couldn't remember.

Oh well. It'd come back to him later.

They always did, eventually.

THE WORLD WAS a complicated place, with a lot of simultaneously running parts keeping everything in balance. He knew all about that when his mother died and his father dumped him off on his aunt—

What the hell? He hadn't thought about his childhood in years. Why was he dredging up old things now? None of it mattered. They were in the past, and though some shrinks may say otherwise, Beckard didn't blame any of this on the people who had given him life. Back in school, one of his professors used to say some people were born with the evil gene. Beckard didn't think he was evil, per se, but maybe he enjoyed things other people didn't, and as a result, that made him...different.

Who the hell cares?

He had to deal with the moment. The now.

And right now, he had very immediate troubles on his hands.

It was probably too much to hope that he could make it back to the bunker unscathed. It had to be Harper. The sergeant was moving a lot faster than Beckard had anticipated. A part of him wasn't entirely surprised. Harper had always been the dedicated cop, the man all the kids fresh out of the academy looked up to. Except for Beckard, of course. Harper reminded him too much of his father—

Concentrate on the now, you idiot!

The swirling lights flashing across the road in front of him were from a makeshift roadblock, essentially one cruiser parked along the shoulder. Beckard saw it too late and even as he stepped on the brake and let the Crown Vic sit idle in the middle of the road, he knew the trooper had already spotted him. It was impossible not to, given the fact he was the only thing traveling on this stretch of road for miles on either side.

A figure stood in the middle of the two lanes waving a flashing wand over his head, trying to get his attention. He was still far enough that the man probably couldn't see him or make out that Beckard was sitting in a squad car.

He glanced up at the rearview mirror, saw nothing but pitch-black behind him.

Screw you, Harper, Beckard thought just before he put the Crown Vic into gear and stepped on the gas.

He moved slowly, gradually, picking up speed as he went.

The trooper was still standing in the middle of the lanes, one hand holding the emergency wand while the other rested on the butt of his sidearm. He was peering forward, trying to get a good look at Beckard, but unable to see much over the bright beams of the headlights blasting into his face.

He pressed down on the gas a little bit more…

The man began waving the wand frantically in the air. The trooper must have known something was wrong. If he didn't, then he realized it pretty quickly when Beckard gunned the gas while he was still fifty yards away.

The wand fell to the highway, and less than two seconds

later a gunshot rang out. The windshield cracked and Beckard actually heard the bullet *zipping* past his head.

Christ, that was close!

He shoved his foot down on the gas pedal until it slammed into the floor and the sedan shot forward like a missile.

Bang! Another bullet smashed through the windshield and drilled a neat hole in the upholstery of the front passenger seat.

Bang! A third bullet missed the vehicle entirely, even though at this point Beckard was close—

WHUMP! The front grill hit the moving figure head-on and sent it flying through the air.

Beckard didn't wait to see where the man landed. He kept going, both hands gripping the steering wheel to keep the Crown Vic from swerving off the road post-impact.

His mind spun, processing the facts before him.

Just the facts, ma'am!

The fact that Harper only had one trooper at this roadblock meant he was short on manpower. Not a surprise, given the time of day. That wasn't going to last forever, though. By morning, the entire highway would be crawling with state police. And leaving the body behind would signal to them that he was in the area. If he was lucky, Harper would assume he had kept going, which would put him out of the state by sunrise. Only an idiot would remain behind, hiding in a bunker in the woods nearby.

He grinned. Maybe he was an idiot. A *brilliant* idiot.

Was that the pills talking? It was hard to tell, given the last few hours.

Beckard turned his options over in his head as he drove on. A part of him was surprised he wasn't more freaked out. Everything he had worked for since the academy days was gone in one night. But for some reason, he wasn't nearly as angry about that as he thought he would have been when the time finally came.

He reached down and took out the pill bottle and shook out two more of the delightful white stuff.

Oh yeah, that hit the spot...

THERE WAS A chance Harper or one of the other troopers might stumble across the same wooded entrance Beckard was taking now, but that possibility was something he had to live with. His only consolation was that this part of the highway was surrounded by absolutely nothing, with the closest hiking trails and hunting grounds many miles away. The way in was also not on any map and there were no signs to indicate a road, such as it was, even existed. Beckard himself had driven right past it for years before that incident with the lost campers.

Even so, as he arrived back at the bunker entrance, he stood outside the squad car for a moment and tried to see if he could hear any noises that didn't belong, or that weren't there when he left an hour ago.

Voices, a car's engine, anything.

But there was just the sound of the creatures around him. The birds chirping, the smaller animals racing along branches, and the much bigger ones darting in and out of brushes on the ground. The sun was starting to peek through the trees and the warmth was already pushing away last night's chill.

His biggest worry was a hunter getting lost and stumbling

across him by accident. Or maybe another pair of clueless campers...

He shook those thoughts away. If it happened, it would happen. Right now, every minute, every hour was a gift that he had to take advantage of. If they found him, then they found him. Until then, he would make it count.

Cool as a cucumber, remember?

Beckard grabbed the bags out of the back seat and headed to the bunker. Pushing the door open was a pain in the ass, and he had to put his left shoulder into it. His entire right side tingled, but he gritted his teeth and sucked it in. Nothing good in this world came without a little pain. He had learned that a long time ago—

Something heavy hit him in the back of the head and Beckard stumbled forward, more stunned than hurt, though he hurt a little bit, too.

What looked like sparks *(sparks?)* showered the air around him as he fell—falling, he was *falling!*—down the stairs.

CHAPTER 21

POLICE HANDCUFFS CONSIST of two cheek plates and the chain in the middle that connects them. The cheek plates themselves make up only half of the rings used to secure the captive's wrists. The other half is the single strand, its end consisting of the ratchet that includes the "teeth" that is pushed into the plate in order to lock the device. This is what makes the *clink-clink* noise when a pair of handcuffs is secured. If properly locked, the teeth go all the way in, leaving no wiggling room for the captured wrist. It also hurt like a sonofabitch, but that's the price of being a criminal.

Of course, when you toss the handcuffs to someone and don't pay attention, it's easy for him (or her) to *not* push the ratchet all the way in, thus leaving the handcuffs with a generous space for someone with slim hands to slide out of.

Like most women, Allie had slim hands. It was one of the reasons why it took her so long to become comfortable with handling weapons. "Girly hands," one of her instructors called them. So when Beckard told her to cuff herself back inside the interrogation room, she did, just not *all the way*. Thank God he was too busy listening for signs of his fellow troopers out in the hallway to notice anything more than the *clink-clink* noise he had expected to hear (and did), and seconds later, the sight of her hands visibly secured as she stood across the table from him.

To keep Beckard from noticing, Allie hadn't done anything to make him inspect her hands up close. He had believed her, because in fact the handcuffs were around her wrists and they did hurt, but they weren't as all the way in as they could have been.

After that, she bided her time. Her best chance of escape was at the state police building, but that wouldn't have worked. Beckard had made it perfectly clear he was willing to kill her if faced with capture. She believed him, too. This was a man who had murdered countless women, including her sister, in the last ten years. What was one more to him? She wanted Beckard dead in the worst way, but she didn't want to die herself. Revenge was only sweet if you were alive to savor it.

When he gave her an extra pair of handcuffs and told her to "chain-link" herself to the metal spike in the bunker, Allie was worried. Beckard had proven himself unpredictable, and she wasn't sure what he was going to do next.

But then he left, and she knew that was her chance. Maybe her only chance.

The only thing she wasn't prepared for was the blood. There was a lot of it. All hers.

She started working on freeing herself five minutes after he closed the bunker door. Girly hands or not, it was far from easy. Her left hand was covered in blood, the skin along the thumb and pinky fingers raw and bleeding by the time she managed to pull the hand completely free of the encircling steel. She could barely hold her mangled hand up and felt sick to her stomach at the sight of so much blood dripping to the concrete floor.

Ten years of research, six years of training, and three years of getting ready for this moment, and I'm going to die from blood loss inside a stinking old bomb shelter from the fifties.

She fought back the nausea and went to work on her right hand.

A part of her thought it would be easier now that she had managed the left, but it wasn't. If anything, it was more difficult because she knew what to expect—pain, blood, and tearing skin. She spent every second of it trying not to pass out and was able to do so by closing her eyes. That way, she didn't actually have to see what she was doing to her hand. If she had a stick, she would have bitten down on it. But she didn't, so Allie thought about Carmen instead.

Her little sister. Beautiful, vivacious, and so talented. Carmen would have been a dancer. A singer. An actress. Maybe all three, as long as it showed off the free spirit that she was, that Allie knew her to be.

Her little sister. Dead now, ten years gone.

And the man responsible could be coming back for her at any moment.

Maybe ten minutes.

Maybe twenty.

An hour?

But he was coming back, and she had to be ready.

Ten years of research, six years of training, and three years of getting ready for this moment, Carmen. I won't let you down. I swear I won't let you down.

Her right hand slipped out of the handcuff with a soft and sickening *plop* and she crumpled to the floor, where she lay on her back and tried to control her ragged breathing. Both her hands were bleeding, and terrible pain pulsed through every finger and every inch of torn and bleeding skin.

She didn't want to move any part of her body, not even when she felt the wetness pooling under her.

Blood. Hers.

It was sticky. She had no idea blood would be that sticky...

No, no, no!

She sat up on the floor gasping, feeling as if the filthy walls had collapsed in on her, making the simple act of breathing a monumental task. It took a few moments before she could calm herself down and confirm she wasn't dead, and that the light shining in her face wasn't the entry to the afterlife.

The pain brought her back to the moment, and Allie glanced down at her bloodied hands and stared at them for the longest time.

The exposed skin at the edges of both hands were red and raw, and the thick layer of blood that covered them were still wet so she couldn't have been unconscious for that long, though she wouldn't have known that by the generous amount of plasma pooling under her. Both her pants and shirt were sticky with blood, and there was a smell in the room that wasn't there when her eyes were last open.

She slowly stood up, careful not to use her hands as crutches. The sight of ruined skin (was that bone underneath?) made her want to gag all over again, and it was only through a lot of effort that she managed to hold everything in. Her stomach was too light, and she realized, almost as an afterthought, that she hadn't eaten anything since yesterday's lunch.

Her hands…had she permanently damaged them? All of this was going to be for nothing if she couldn't use them again, especially when he came back—

She froze.

That noise!

It was barely audible, but clearly the same low rumbling she had heard earlier when Beckard left in the Crown Vic.

Beckard. He was back!

How long had she been unconscious? Ten minutes? Thirty? An *hour?*

She needed a weapon. *Any* weapon.

She glanced back at the handcuffs hanging off the metal spike. The long, sharp metal would have made a fine weapon (she imagined shoving it through Beckard's skull), but that would mean prying it loose from the wall. She couldn't have done that even with good hands, and right now…

Blood. Hers. Dripping from the handcuffs.

She almost threw up at the sight, but managed to get a hold of herself at the very last moment because—

The vibrations along the bunker's concrete walls had stopped, which meant Beckard had parked the car and turned off the engine.

Find a weapon! Any weapon!

The cot was no good. Bashing Beckard's head in with a fluffy (albeit nasty and stained) mattress wasn't going to work. No, she needed something solid, firm, and maybe—

It was right in front of her the entire time and was the only reason she wasn't standing in darkness at the moment: one of the portable LED lamps hanging off the wall from a hook.

She grabbed it, wincing at the contact of the lamp's plastic handle against her still-bleeding fingers. Every inch of her hands hurt, as if she was constantly being shocked with electricity. She grimaced her way through them and thought about Carmen instead.

Her little sister. Everyone who had ever met Carmen loved her. You couldn't help yourself. She was kind and giving and beautiful. So beautiful. Even in a hundred years, Allie would never come close to matching her little sister's—

The harsh grinding of the door opening behind her snapped her back again.

She raced up the steps, dripping blood the entire way but refusing to acknowledge it. What was one or a dozen more drips when her clothes were still damp from lying down earlier? She imagined she must look like the girl in the movie *Carrie*, at the prom, covered in pig's blood.

She reached the top landing when the door was halfway open. Beckard was slightly bent over and had his shoulder pressed against the door, so his back was partially turned to her as she hurried up the steps and slid, gasping for breath (and praying he didn't hear), behind the moving thick slab of wood.

He was holding two large bulging plastic bags in his good hand, while a third smaller bag dangled from his heavily bandaged one. He stood in the open door for a moment to catch his breath, which came out shallow and labored, and for a split second she took pleasure in knowing he was probably in nearly as much pain as she was at the moment.

She tightened her grip around the lamp's handle, grimacing

at the searing pain that caused, as he straightened up and stepped through the door, exposing his left side to her. Unfortunately that meant his holstered Glock was on the other side, and she wanted that gun. The knife was facing her and within easier reach, but she wanted that gun. She *needed* that gun.

With no choice, she swung the lamp and caught him in the back of the head.

He might have let out a guttural grunt just before he stumbled forward, the LED lightbulbs popping and showering the landing with sparks. As his body moved away from her, she dropped the lamp and followed and reached for the handle of the gun in the holster—

No! her mind screamed as Beckard tripped on the top step and went tumbling down one, two—ten steps to the bottom of the landing.

Desperation and regret quickly gave way to optimism at the sight of him crumpled down there like a pretzel.

Maybe that did it. Maybe he broke his neck. Did I hear a crack? Maybe...

She took the first step down after him when he opened his eyes and looked back up at her from the concrete floor below, his body wedged at the turn. He was on his back and the bags he had been carrying had gone flying. Food, drinks, and some cheap off-the-rack T-shirts and a cap were scattered around him.

Then he was reaching for the Glock—

She turned and fled and heard the *bang!* as Beckard fired behind her.

A big chunk of the concrete wall above the door exploded and showered her as she ran through the falling debris.

Another *bang!* but this one didn't do anything, because she was already outside and running through the glowing dawn. The woods seemed to have come alive and birds were chirping wildly from the trees. She swore there were animals running around the underbrush and bushes to the left and right of her.

The police car was close by, and she made a beeline for it. There were two bullet holes in the windshield that hadn't been there earlier. What did that mean? Had Harper caught up to Beckard while he was out there? Was the state police sergeant on his way here now? Maybe she should hunker down and wait for him. Maybe—

The shotgun!

It leaned between the two front seats, but even as she lunged for the door, she knew it wouldn't open. She jerked on the handle anyway—ignoring the screaming pain from the contact of her raw and bleeding fingers against the cold metal—just to be sure.

The door wouldn't budge.

She thought about breaking the window.

How? With her hands? What hands?

With her elbows? Her feet?

If she could find something stronger—a rock, maybe—she might be able to gain access. Of course, she'd need time for that, which was something she didn't have at the moment.

She ran past the car and saw the rough trail Beckard had carved out for himself with his travels back and forth from the bunker. It was barely noticeable, but the trampled grass told her where to go. Or, at least, the direction.

Allie didn't run down the road. Instead, she darted into the thick patch of woods alongside it and burst into the trees, lifting her arms over her head like a shield to batter away branches in her path.

There was just enough light for her to see where she was going. All she had to do was keep following the road while staying out of sight. Eventually, it would take her back to the highway. Harper would have mobilized the state police by now and would be looking for them. There would be cops on the road. She might not have needed—or wanted—them last night, but she could use one (or a dozen) of them right about now.

She wasn't sure how long she had been running when she saw it—a large bump lying in front of her, like some creature that had dug its way out of the ground to block her path. Her instincts were to jump over it, but knowing what she should have done and actually doing it were two different things. Her body was tired and her hands *hurt so damn much*, and she ended up tripping on it instead. Allie stumbled forward but still managed to turn her entire body, ending up on the slightly damp ground on her butt.

She stared forward at the body. It was the state trooper she had seen in the backseat of the squad car when Beckard first put her inside. Jones something. She hadn't seen it last time, but in the growing daylight the gaping hole in the back of his head, facing her, was hard to miss.

Allie scrambled to her feet and started off again, but she hadn't gone very far when she stopped and looked back at Jones.

Weapons. She needed weapons!

But Jones didn't have one to give her. He was unarmed and wasn't even wearing his gun belt. Instead, she began unbuttoning his khaki shirt, when—

"Allie!"

The only reason she didn't get up right away and race off,

Jones's shirt be damned, was the realization that Beckard's voice was coming from a distance. Though near enough she could hear it echoing across the woods, she concluded he was still back at the bunker. That helped her to finish unbuttoning Jones's shirt.

"You can run, but you can't hide!" he shouted.

Who says I'm hiding, asshole?

She pulled Jones's shirt off and staggered up to her feet a second time and turned and began jogging through the woods. She ripped the shirt apart as she went, then began wrapping the pieces around her damaged hands. The feel of the soft fabric cocooning her raw skin stung briefly before becoming a soothing glove.

After about thirty more yards of constantly moving, she could barely feel the pain anymore.

Or, at least, that's what she told herself.

CHAPTER 22

HE DIDN'T KNOW what hurt more, getting hit in the head with the lamp or rolling down ten concrete steps and landing on the back of his neck. Of course, he didn't have time to really turn over the options before he saw her standing at the top of the stairs, halfway between following him down (for his gun, no doubt) or fleeing.

He helped her with that decision by groping for the sidearm, then switching the gun over to his left hand and taking a shot at her. Thank God Glocks didn't come with safeties, otherwise he would have spent another second trying to find the switch. Of course, even without wasting that extra time, his first shot still went awry, smashing into the wall above the door.

Not even close!

He had been wondering all day if he could hit the broad side of a barn with his left hand. Now he knew.

Then she was gone, fleeing through the door.

He didn't know why, but he fired a second shot after her anyway. Maybe it was frustration or anger or—oh, who was he kidding. It was anger. Simple, pissed-off anger. At that moment, he stopped caring about using her as his final swan song, and he just wanted her dead. Too bad she wasn't cooperating.

Beckard pushed himself up from the hard ground with a lot of effort. A bag of chips that had landed on his stomach fell and he stepped on it with his boots. There was blood all over the steps, and for a moment he thought it was his.

He checked, but he wasn't bleeding. At least, not outside his bandages. His neck hurt and his back felt like someone had landed a train on top of it, and every part of his legs and arms and joints shivered with every movement he made. But he wasn't bleeding.

So where did all the blood come from? And how the hell had she gotten out of the handcuffs?

Then he remembered the sight of her hands. Bloodied.

He stumbled down the steps and turned the corner and saw the handcuffs dangling from the metal spike in the wall. Blood was still dripping from them.

Beckard turned around and started up the steps again. He *crunched* a package of Snowballs and kicked a bottle of Gatorade out of his path. He had wanted this to go down a different way, but well, nothing was really going as planned these days anyway, so why should this be any different? He had adjusted on the fly before, and he'd just have to do it again.

No muss, no fuss.

He knew she wasn't going to be outside waiting to bash his head in a second time. Not the way she was running. No, she'd look for a weapon. A smart girl like her would go right for the car. But he had locked it (old habits die hard, even out here in the middle of nowhere) so she wouldn't get anything there. He expected her to at least try to break the window, get at the shotgun inside, but the Crown Vic looked intact when he stepped out of the bunker.

He stopped for a moment and glanced around. A generous dose of warm orange was spreading above the tree crowns and filling up large sections of the wood with slivers of light.

He checked his watch to be sure: 5:45 A.M.

It wouldn't be long now. Half an hour before the sun came up completely and the world woke up. It would be another hour, maybe two, until Harper got the manpower he needed to put in all the roadblocks up and down the highway, seal off the state, and pray he hadn't already made it out hours earlier. By now, Harper would have torn Thomas Beckard's life upside down. The banks, the credit cards—all those would be frozen by the end of the day.

Ten years. Not a bad run...

"Allie!" he shouted at the top of his lungs.

He listened to his own voice echoing off the trees, scattering birds nearby.

"You can run, but you can't hide!"

She didn't answer. Of course not. She'd be running by now. Where to? That was the question.

And the answer was easy.

The highway. A smart girl like her would recognize the barely-there road at the end of the clearing. There wasn't much, but enough to get a firm direction of where civilization lay.

It didn't take him long to spot the fresh bloody drops on the ground leading into the woods. That made him grin to himself. It was just last night when she had been tracking *him* using the same method.

He slipped in through two towering trees in pursuit.

BECKARD WAS FEELING giddy, which explained why he had just chuckled at the sight of Jones lying in the grass sans shirt. Someone had been rummaging through the poor trooper's dead body, and it wasn't the animals.

What were you looking for, Allie?

He remembered the sight of her hands dripping blood. Taking Jones's shirt also explained why the blood trail he had been following for the last few minutes had suddenly dried up past Jones's body.

Smart. Really smart girl.

She wasn't completely invisible yet, though. He could still make out the trampled grass she had left in her wake.

He turned to follow that trail now when he stopped and almost fell. He stuck out his hand and by a stroke of luck found a tree nearby to keep himself upright. A wave of nausea rushed through him, followed by lightheadedness.

The pills. He had taken too many of them.

He tried to shake it off, but that only made things worse. Beckard sat down, leaned against the gnarled face of the tree, and snapped his eyes shut to rest.

He didn't know how long he sat there, not moving. It could have been a few seconds, a few minutes, or maybe—an hour? No, it couldn't have been an hour. When he opened his eyes again, it was still dawn and sunlight was still fighting to spread across the sky above him.

Still early morning, so it hadn't been that long.

He pushed up from the ground and stumbled forward, gripping the Glock in his left hand. His right was held together by stitches underneath the almost cast-like bandages and was numbed all over. His face, thank God, had stopped hurting. Or, at least, he couldn't feel the broken nose anymore. He wasn't entirely sure if that was a good thing, but at the moment he was grateful for one less pulsating pain to worry about.

Beckard pushed on. It was almost over anyway. Once he found her, he'd finish it. He had wanted to prolong this, savor his last hurrah, but there was no chance of that now. She was becoming too dangerous and too time-consuming.

"Allie!" he shouted. "I think we got off on the wrong foot. Let's talk this out! That highway's not going to get any closer!"

There was no response. But then, he didn't expect her to answer him. She'd be making her way toward the road at the moment. How much of a head start did she have on him? It depended on how long he had actually slept when he closed his eyes a few minutes ago.

"Fine!" he shouted. "Have it your way!"

He continued following the obvious signs across the trampled grass. He was actually a little surprised she hadn't taken more care with her footsteps. Maybe he had overestimated her. She had probably lived in the cities all of her life, after all. So did all the other women he had taken over the years. They were delicate things, bred for busy sidewalks and intersections and cafés and offices. Most of them were tough, yes, but city tough was different from country tough. They had all found that out eventually.

Even Allie, for all her preparations. When you got right down to it, she was more equipped to survive in the cities than out here. In the woods, she might as well be a drunk babe walking around trampling everything in sight. As smart as she clearly was, he had no trouble picking up her trail.

In fact, it almost felt as if she wasn't even making any efforts to disguise herself, almost as if she was doing it on purpose—

He froze.

No.

Could it be? Could she really be *that* smart?

Had he overestimated her intelligence, or underestimated it?

Could all of this just be...

Oh, shit.

CHAPTER 23

IT WAS THE biggest weapon she could find in the little time that she had. Two feet long (or, well, twenty-six inches, if she wanted to be terribly specific about it) and four inches wide. It was heavy enough that when she broke it off the biggest tree she could find in the immediate area, she almost dropped it because its heft surprised her.

Her bloodied hands, despite being swaddled in ripped pieces of the dead state trooper's shirt, screamed like wildfire as she tightened her double grip along the lower half of the branch, choking up on it as if she were about to wield a baseball bat.

Swing for the fences, girl.

For Carmen...

And he walked right past her, just like she knew he would. He might have been stumbling a bit, maybe even swaying slightly. That might have been the result of the pills he was wolfing down like candy to stave off the pain of last night. Either way, she took it as a good sign that he was unsteady on his feet, which did wonders to convince her that they were on almost equal ground.

If only she could get that gun out of his hand...

He couldn't see her because she was well hidden, having circled back from the trail she had left in her wake to crouch behind a bush. A series of big and obvious (and oh so very "loud") footsteps that led him here.

When he stopped ten feet in front of her and stared down at her tracks, she knew almost instantly that he had figured it out. He was lifting his head and starting to look around when she jumped to her feet and burst out of the bush, both hands cocking the heavy branch back, back, *back*—

He saw her and his eyes widened, and he might have even started to say something, but he never got it out because she hit him square in the right leg. She was aiming for the kneecap, but she landed just a bit too high and hit his thigh instead. The blow was still effective and he looked as if he was going to topple. Somehow, he managed to remain upright.

For a while, anyway.

She swung again and heard the very satisfying *crack!* as the branch hit and shattered against the Glock in his left hand. He had been in the process of raising it to shoot her when she landed the second swing. The gun flew out of his hand and he grunted, clenching his teeth in either frustration or pain; she didn't know or care at the moment.

She expected him to leap for the fallen gun, or turn and flee. After all, she had the upper hand.

She was wrong, because he attacked instead.

He moved pretty fast for a man whose right arm was hanging at his side like a useless piece of meat. Then again, he was swinging with his left hand, the fingers tightening into a ball at the same moment it smashed into her chest.

Pain exploded across Allie's vision. Beckard might have been operating at only fifty percent (or below), but she had clearly underestimated the man's strength because the blow stunned her and she staggered back, fighting to regain her balance. She had taken three steps backward when Beckard let out a ferocious scream and lunged at her.

She swung again with the branch. It was mostly a defensive reaction on her part, but it prompted him to instinctively lift his right arm in an attempt to ward it off. The branch *cracked!* on contact and broke in half.

Beckard let out a howl that sounded more animal than human.

Allie thought he would retreat after *that*, but again, she was very wrong. The man must have been drawing from some deep reservoir of willpower, because he kept coming. She didn't know if he couldn't feel the pain that must have been rippling through his right arm at the moment or if he had just somehow chosen to ignore it.

He rammed his shoulder into her chest like a bulldozer. There was nothing elegant or strategic about it. He was bigger and heavier, and he was probably overconfident that he could knock her down with sheer brutality. And he was right.

They both tumbled to the ground with his much heavier body collapsing on top of her. A split second after her back slammed into the earth, the sky seemed to cave in on top of her in a blinding rush.

He was crushing her with his body, and she knew right away that physically grabbing and throwing him off wasn't going to be possible. She had learned a long time ago that regardless of how prepared she was for a fight—physically and mentally—a man would always have the advantage over her when they were in close proximity. Which was why she didn't bother wasting energy trying to push him off her and instead began whaling on his head with the remaining piece of branch still clutched in her hand.

The stick felt much lighter now without its other half, but it was still heavy enough to do some damage. She hit him once, twice—*three times* in the side of the head, and each time chunks of the branch broke free. She couldn't have landed a fourth blow even if she had wanted to because by then the branch had literally fallen apart in her hand like a brittle piece of candy until she was just holding onto a piece of twig.

Blood was pouring down the side of his face, and she swore it only made him look more primal. Which she thought was ironic; she had never looked at him as a man but always as a beast that needed to be put down. That was how she had approached this mission, how she knew she could pull the trigger when the time came—

Trigger.

Gun.

Where's the Glock?

Something wet landed on her cheek, and Allie almost threw up. It was Beckard's blood, pouring down in thick rivulets from the gash along his temple and onto her. Some had streamed around his left eye socket and pooled there, making his eye look bloodshot. It was a sight to behold—one side perfectly normal while the other was fiery red, like something you'd see on the face of a demon from the pits of hell.

Allie was trying to fight through the revulsion of being bathed in Beckard's blood when a streak of sunlight glinted off the sharp blade of a knife. He had pulled out the knife along his hip and was raising it over his head and was grinning down at her like a wild animal, blood running along the side of his face to his jawline, then *drip-drip-dripping* onto her.

"You wanna know what Carmen said before I killed her?" he asked, though every word came out sounding more like pained grunts. "She begged me not to do it. She cried and cried and cried. I got so tired of it I cut her throat just to shut her the hell up!"

She was waiting for it. Gathering her strength and loosening up her body. Her arms were flat on the ground, not fighting him. If he noticed that she wasn't resisting his much heavier body as it pinned her, he didn't show it.

Then again, she wasn't sure if he was aware of anything at the moment but his own clearly maniacal emotions. He certainly hadn't recognized that his entire right hand had begun bleeding again, that the white gauze was getting redder by the second. Was he even remotely aware that he was losing an obscene amount of blood, so much that he could actually bleed to death out here?

She stopped thinking about him and thought of Carmen instead.

Ten years of research, little sister. Six years of training and three years of getting ready for this one single moment.

This is for you, Carmen.

God help me if I time it wrong.

He plunged the knife down, aiming it straight for her neck. Just like she knew he would, because Beckard always went for the neck. All those grisly crime scene photos from his earlier years, and then later when he tried to hide his pattern, but they were there if you knew where to look, and she knew where to look.

The killing blow always goes to the neck!

She jerked her relaxed body to the right, twisting her torso at the same instant. The knife flashed by a split second later and sank into the ground, just barely half an inch from her neck. He had driven the blade down with such force that it kept going and didn't stop until the guard *thumped!* against the floor of the woods.

Allie didn't give him time to adjust, to pull the knife out. She balled her right hand into a fist and swung at his face, aiming for the spot along his temple where he was bleeding profusely. He had bent slightly over her body, his forward momentum carrying him so much closer to her that she didn't even have to rise from the ground to make contact.

She felt the *crunch* of her knuckles slamming home against the side of his face. A thick wad of blood sprayed the area and splashed her at the same time. She flinched, blinked out the blood that had splattered her eyes, and refocused on her target through her suddenly red-tinted vision.

Again! Again!

She ignored the warm sensation of *(his)* blood on her face and hit him again, and again, and *again*, all while he was still trying to pull the knife out of the ground. He was grimacing with the pain—or was that confusion on his face? Did he suddenly understand what was happening now? That although he was on top of her and he was bigger and stronger, that he was no longer in charge? That she was? That soon—

The fifth time she smashed her fist into the side of his face, he finally relented and toppled off her like some kind of sleeping bear, unable to remain upright any longer.

Allie didn't wait, didn't hesitate, didn't spend a precious second or two wondering if he was hurt enough that he would stay down. She broke into motion, rolling to her right, and didn't stop until she was winded and pain throbbed from her side where her broken ribs reminded her they still needed medical attention.

She scrambled up to her knees and looked for the gun. Beckard's gun.

Where the hell did it go? If it had fallen into one of the bushes, she was out of luck. There was no way she was going to find it in all of this green—

There!

It was fifteen feet away from her and *five feet behind Beckard.* Except Beckard was too busy pushing himself up from the earth, dripping blood from one entire half of his face, to know what was back there. He was a truly sorry sight, and she might have actually felt some sympathy for him if the last ten years of her life hadn't been devoted to ending his miserable existence.

She ran for the gun.

He was still trying desperately to pull the knife out of the ground when he looked up and saw her running toward him. More than that, he saw where her eyes were looking, and he turned around, saw the gun, and gave up on the knife. He dived for the Glock, stretching out with his bloodied right hand with an almost guttural grunt.

She was still three feet away when he wrapped his fingers around the gun—

No, no, no!

She was moving on pure instinct when she veered off target at the last second and turned slightly to her left just before launching her body forward again, but this time feetfirst. She aimed for the biggest target—his chest—and slammed both shoes into it with everything she had.

He was swinging the Glock around when she caught him with both flying feet and sent him reeling back to the ground. She was hoping she could jar the gun loose, but Beckard somehow clung onto it even as he fell. She landed back down to earth on her ass and back, her body vibrating from head to toe from the impact. She wanted to scream out but couldn't manage that much. The pain from her broken ribs was excruciating, and she wondered if that little stunt hurt her more than it did him.

Beckard was on his back and sitting up slowly. So she had managed to hurt him after all, though not enough to make him give up the gun. What was it going to take to put this monster down? The gun still clutched in his fist, she thought, might go a long way in achieving that end. Except the semiautomatic was in *his* hand and not *hers*, which was a big problem.

He turned his head and grinned at her through a mask of his own blood. She stared back at him because there was no point in moving anyway. He had her. The gun in his right hand was pointed across his chest and right at her from five feet away. Just getting up and running would have taken two, maybe three seconds. She had less than one at the moment.

It was no use. He had her.

Dead to rights.

I'm sorry, Carmen, I failed.

Please forgive me...

She thought he might say something clever—or at least something he thought was clever—before he shot her, but he didn't. Instead, he just fired—

—and she felt a sharp sting as the bullet *buzzed* past her.

The sudden jolt of pain came from her right ear, the sensation like getting stung by a bee, as the bullet *clipped* her.

There was the look of surprise on his face, shock that he had missed her from less than five feet away. Maybe it was the fact that he was using his heavily bandaged hand to hold the gun, which couldn't handle the recoil in its current condition. She didn't know and didn't particularly care, because *she was alive!*

Beckard attempted to stand up when she lunged at him, throwing herself forward, headfirst this time. He saw her coming and fired a second shot—

And missed again!

This time he fired so quickly that the bullet went wide, even as she barreled into him with everything she had and knocked both of them back to the ground again. He struggled under her, his much bigger body already getting into position to throw her off. Before he could do that, she grabbed the gun by the barrel with both hands and rolled off him. He let out a piercing scream as she twisted the gun and broke his finger in the trigger guard in the process.

She might have also screamed right along with him as every inch of her hands throbbed with misery under the swaddling, even as she tightened her fingers around the barrel and jerked it with everything she had until it slid out of his stubborn grip.

Allie landed in a pile next to him and kept rolling until she was sure she had enough space between them. She scrambled up, managing to get to her knees even as he mirrored her actions four feet away.

She heard rather than felt the blood dripping from her right ear, where his first shot had taken a big chunk. Every inch of her hands vibrated, currents of pain rippling from every single one of her fingertips. She tried not to think about what she looked like at the moment and focused on controlling her breathing instead. It wasn't nearly as easy to shoot a man with a handgun, even from a few feet away. Despite her best efforts, though, it felt like a train was rumbling across her chest.

If she thought she looked miserable, Beckard was in even worse shape. He was cradling his broken finger, his face covered in a thick film of pain and fury and blood. Eyes—one bloodshot, the other normal—glared back at her as if he couldn't quite believe what had happened, or what was happening.

She stared back at him, the Glock in both hands, and aimed at his head.

"No," he gasped.

"No?" she repeated.

"It can't end this way."

"Why the hell not? What makes you so special?"

"It can't end this way," he said again, as if she hadn't said anything.

"Yes, it can," she said, and blew his brains out with the first shot.

His body—lifeless and empty, a husk of nothing, if he ever was anything to begin with—flopped to the ground and lay perfectly still.

She let the gun fall to her lap because it felt suddenly very heavy, and she just didn't have the strength to keep it raised any longer. The recoil against her mangled hands didn't hurt nearly as much as she had expected, and whatever fight she had in her seemed to evaporate in a rush of expelled air at the sight of his body toppling over and not getting up.

It was over.

Ten years of research, six years of training, and three years of getting ready for this moment...and it was finally over.

There wasn't much of Beckard's head left. With the hole in his forehead and the blood that covered nearly sixty, maybe seventy percent of his face, it was a grotesque sight, the kind that she was sure would give her nightmares for years to come. Even in death, the man would still continue to haunt her.

Allie let out a deep breath and lay down on the earth, letting the Glock fall from her numbed fingers. She stared up past the tree canopies and focused on the clearing sky. It was getting brighter with every second, signaling the coming of a new day.

Somewhere in the distance, she might have heard dogs barking, or maybe that could have just been her imagination.

She decided not to fight the unbearable fatigue and closed her eyes. She went to sleep, forcing herself to think about good things and better times.

Hi, Carmen, it's your big sister.
You can go to sleep now. It's over.
It's all over...

EPILOGUE

SHE WOKE UP in bed.

It was quiet and peaceful, and the mattress under her was soft and comfortable, far from the hard and pricking cot of a prison cell. Both of her hands were heavily bandaged and there was surprisingly very little pain. If anything, she felt numbed all over, although from time to time there was a slight itching sensation from one of her ears. An IV *drip-drip-dripped* next to her bed. The clear liquid inside the bag was probably morphine or a damn fine substitute. A lone machine to her right occasionally *beeped*.

Every now and then she could hear a calm voice over a loudspeaker, and something *clanking* as it rolled past the door to her left. It was almost entirely dark inside the room except for a computer monitor next to a sink and a yellow night-light near the floor in front of her.

"Allie Krycek," a familiar male voice said. "CPA, secretary, waitress, and I believe at one point you even worked as a nanny?"

Allie looked to her right at the man in the state trooper's uniform, sitting on a long uncomfortable sofa next to the windows.

"I guess now we can add 'vigilante' to that list," Harper said.

She could barely make him out in the semidarkness, but there was no mistaking that voice. Harper would have made a great hero in a Hollywood Western.

"How long?" she asked.

"A couple of days. You lost a lot of blood out there."

"How did I get here?"

"We were looking for Beckard in the area when we heard the gunshots. He killed one of my troopers a few miles from where we eventually found you."

"I heard dogs…"

"Apollo found you."

"Apollo?"

"The dog."

She gave him a confused look.

"The one that took a chunk out of Beckard in the cabin. He was helping with the search and picked up your scent. You're lucky we had him out there, otherwise you might have bled to death before we found you in time." He leaned slightly forward. "I'm curious. How long did it take?"

"What?"

"To lure him out."

"Four months, one week, and five days."

Harper chuckled. "Four months. Out there, driving back and forth. You're a pretty impressive woman, Allie."

"I had a lot of time on my hands."

"I bet. If I was looking to hire someone who could do a little of everything, I'd give you a call. I guess when your sole goal in life is to find and kill someone, it doesn't pay to get stuck in a long-term career."

She wasn't sure where he was going, and Allie was too tired to care. "Am I under arrest?"

"Now what would you be under arrest for?"

"Beckard."

"You're a hero. The state police don't arrest heroes."

Hero?

She wanted to laugh but didn't have the strength to do even that. She said instead, "I was right. Beckard is the Roadside Killer."

"Was, yeah. We've been turning his life inside out. Everything he was, everything he did…we know everything there is to know. There's no doubt that he is—was—the Roadside Killer, and that he kept on killing long after we stopped looking for him. The national media is burning us alive at the stakes for that." He sighed. "I guess we had it coming."

"Do they know…?"

"About you? Yes and no."

"Meaning?"

"They know you're involved and that you were the one who killed him. But they don't know everything. We made the decision not to tell them everything."

"I was just another victim…"

"Yes. A vigilante would make great news copy, but it's not going to be good for any of us, you included."

"You said 'we' made the decision. Who is 'we'?"

"Me. My commanding officer. His commanding officer. The governor. *We.* There's going to be rumors, and some people won't be able to keep their mouths shut. The media will ask and ask, but we'll just keep denying it. Obviously, all of it depends on you."

"Me…"

"Do you agree that it's better for everyone if no one knew what you did out here? I mean, the truth. The whole truth?"

She smiled. "You won't get any arguments from me."

"Good. I'll let my superiors know you're on board. They're going to be very relieved."

"So it's over…"

"It's over."

He smiled at her, and Allie just barely had the energy to return it.

"What now?" Harper asked.

"What do you mean?"

"What are you going to do now that it's over? That Beckard's in the ground?"

"I don't understand…"

Harper looked amused. "How long have you been hunting Beckard, Allie?"

"A decade…"

"And in all that time, didn't you ever wonder what you'd do after it was over?"

She opened her mouth to answer…but nothing came out.

Instead, Allie lay still and looked up at the ceiling, turning the question over in her head.

Finally, she said, "I don't know. I didn't think I'd be alive to even worry about what I'd do after this was all over."

Harper stood up from the sofa. "Well, you got through it alive, Allie Krycek. After we introduce you to the media and everyone plays their part, you'll have plenty of time to figure out what to do with the rest of your life."

She watched him walk across the room and to the door. "Just like that?"

"Just like that." The state trooper looked back at her, his pleasant smile visible against the glowing computer monitor nearby. "Get some rest. We have a long week ahead of us. I'll be back with a couple of other people to get our stories straight in the coming days."

"What about the kids? Rachel and Wade?"

"I've already talked to them and we came to an understanding, too. We're going to keep their names out of the reports and from the media for as long as we can. They're college kids. The last thing they want is to be associated with this for the rest of their lives." The sergeant opened the door. "Get some rest, Allie. You deserve it."

"What about the dog?"

"The dog?"

"What's going to happen to Apollo?"

He shrugged. "He needs a new owner. When you're up and walking again, swing by the pound and reintroduce yourself to him."

He stepped outside and closed the door after him.

Allie looked after him for a moment before turning away and closing her eyes. She wasn't really tired, but there was something about being in a hospital bed with a needle sticking out of her arm that made her sleepy. Sleep didn't come right away, though. Instead, she asked herself the same question Harper had asked her.

What's next?

For the first time in a long time, she didn't dream about death and murder and blood.

She dreamt about Carmen instead.

They were young again. Carmen was happy and dancing, because there was nothing in this world she loved more than to dance. Which worked out for the both of them, because there was nothing in this world Allie loved more than to see Carmen happy...

Made in the USA
Middletown, DE
26 September 2015